BETWEEN TWO WORLDS

A new family takes a lot of getting used to...

When fourteen-year-old Chloë Brannigan's mum Shelly gets married again, Chloë has to get used to a ready-made family, as her step-father Ed Wright has four children of his own. Moving into their house, Chloë finds it alien at first, but gradually realises compromises have to be made. In fact, it's not just Chloë who has some adjusting to do, as her stay-at-home father Kenny finds out when his new girlfriend Philly wants to go travelling! Even her mum becomes torn between career and family, when an accident makes them all think about what is most important to them.

BETWEEN TWO WORLDS

by

Sue Moorcroft

Dales Large Print Books
Long Preston, North Yorkshire,
BD23 4ND, England.

British Library Cataloguing in Publication Data.

Moorcroft, Sue
    Between two worlds.

    A catalogue record of this book is
    available from the British Library

    ISBN   978-1-84262-693-1 pbk

First published in Great Britain in 2007
by D. C. Thomson & Co. Ltd.

Copyright © Sue Moorcroft 2007

Cover illustration © Len Thurston by arrangement with
P.W.A. International Ltd.

The moral right of the author has been asserted

Published in Large Print 2009 by arrangement with
Sue Moorcroft, care of MBA Literary Agents

Dales Large Print is an imprint of Library Magna Books Ltd.

Printed and bound in Great Britain by
T.J. (International) Ltd., Cornwall, PL28 8RW

Chapter One

Wedding Bells

She was late, and she'd promised she wouldn't be. Her mum was going to go bananas!

Chloë Brannigan raced up the Avenue and into the drive of the Old Manse, gravel spurting from beneath the trainers on her flying feet, shrubs shaking the remainder of an early morning shower from their waxy green leaves.

The house was decorated, ready for the wedding reception. Pots of perfect ivory lilies lined the gravel and an enormous swag of white satin threaded with dusky pink and gold ribbon billowed above the imposing portico.

At the glossy black front door, Chloë slid to a halt and lifted her hand to the ornate doorknob. She wavered. Then she reached for the bell push. Almost immediately, the door swung open.

'Why on earth did you ring?' Seventeen-year-old Jason, soon to be her stepbrother, towered from the top step.

He was the oldest of Ed's four children, Jason, Melissa, Emily and Patrick. Three years her senior, he was also a footballer.

'You're supposed to live here now, remember?' He grinned.

Chloë pulled an agonised face.

'Is Mum—'

'Having a hissy fit because you're late? Yes. Loudly.'

Groaning, Chloë ducked under his arm and ran for the elegant sweep of the broad oak staircase. Once up, she hesitated at the door to the room that was to be hers before stepping inside.

Her room. She gazed at the gold-star-spangled wallpaper and russet velvet curtains.

Even though she'd chosen the décor, it didn't feel like her room. It was unnaturally tidy, for one thing. No paints, pencils or pads; she was supposed to move all that stuff in next week.

She wished she could sit down now with a pencil, or perhaps her watercolours and inks. She could lose herself in the translucent colours and the smell of fresh paper...

'Chloë!'

She leaped to face the door, still panting. 'Oh, Mum, I'm so sorry! I did run all the way. Dad's alarm didn't go off, and then the car got temperamental.'

Shelly, Chloë's mother, looked far from her usual unadorned self. Her blonde hair was professionally arranged in an extravagance of curls caught up with fresh flowers, she was fully made-up and manicured – but still belted into a navy towelling robe. She tutted at Chloë, but also smiled.

'At least you're here now. That blessed old car! I know all about it; your dad phoned to explain. I should never have agreed to you staying with him last night, with the wedding party due to leave from here. But at least you've made it in time to get your hair done – so hurry!'

Two minutes under the shower, then Chloë was herded into a chair for her long, glossy brown hair to be blow-dried rapidly, whisked up on the back of her head and stuffed with pink rosebuds. The whole arrangement was then sprayed thoroughly with hair lacquer. It felt tight and stiff and itchy.

But there was no time for adjustments and, after a swipe of special occasion mascara, she wriggled into a ballerina-length cream dress with gold lace panels and a dusky pink sash. She reached behind herself for the zip and began to pull. But it went so far, and no farther.

Rats, this was going to be difficult. She tugged the little metal tag. Then she wiggled it. Then she pulled the zip down and tried again, silently reproaching Ed Wright for wanting a big, formal wedding.

It was to be the kind of affair that Kenny, Chloë's father, called 'a posh do', which meant that Chloë had to be a bridesmaid.

Again, the zip stuck. Precious minutes ticked by as she struggled.

A perfunctory knock, then fifteen-year-old Melissa rustled into the room looking tall, cool and collected in an identical dress, making Chloë feel badly wrapped and gauche in comparison. Maybe it was normal to feel outshone by big sisters? And that went for stepsisters, too?

'Bouquet.' Melissa handed over more pink rosebuds surrounded by a lush fall of fern. 'Everyone's waiting on the landing.'

One sharp tug and she'd zipped Chloë firmly into the dress.

'Let's not hang around.'

Out of breath, Chloë pursued Melissa to the top of the wide, dogleg stairs where the bride's wedding party waited.

8

'I'm ready.'

'Just in time.' Shelly dropped a kiss on Chloë's cheek, and Chloë hugged her mother gently in return, careful of the expensive bridal gown.

'You look pretty,' she whispered.

Not for Shelly lace or beads. She was beautiful in a heavy fall of plain, deep cream satin almost to her ankles, long enough to pool behind her on the staircase as she stepped down, pausing for the benefit of the photographer hovering below.

Melissa, who, probably by virtue of being a year older than Chloë, seemed to have appointed herself chief attendant, passed Shelly her impressive bouquet of cream rosebuds threaded with gold ribbon and fell in behind her, poised as if she slid into this kind of clothing every weekend.

Ten-year-old Emily, however, was not so composed, tripping over her hem and dropping her flowers the instant she tried the stairs in heeled shoes.

'For goodness' sake!' she muttered, snatching at the fabric. 'Does there have to be so much dress? I wish I could've been an usher like Jason and Patrick. At least they got to wear trousers.'

Patrick, the youngest of the Wright children, had shown no signs of being any happier with his top hat than Emily was with her satin.

'And why do the bridesmaids have to be last to the church? I've been hanging around for ages. I could have been doing something! Why was Chloë allowed to turn up at the last moment when I've had to be here all morning?'

'The car's here now,' Shelly said soothingly. Only the trembling of the flowers in her hair betrayed any hint of nerves or excitement. 'Let's go, girls.'

Still out of breath, Chloë felt her heart hammering as it hit her anew that when she got into the long, black wedding car, it would be because her mother was the bride.

Kenny Brannigan walked to the end of Bryant Street where it joined Broadway, the main road through the centre of town.

Arriving at the traffic lights, he hovered, hands in pockets.

He felt foolish, done up in a suit. Double foolish in the midst of the jeans-clad Saturday shoppers, bustling along with their bags. But he didn't intend to miss seeing Chloë in her posh frock, and he certainly wasn't going to lurk about in his jeans and

T-shirt while the wedding party sailed past in their finery.

He waited only a few minutes before the black Rolls Royce purred towards him, slowed by the traffic but stately and gleaming.

And there was Chloë at the window! Her face bore a trace of anxiety as the car slowed for the red light, but the instant she spotted him she broke into her usual happy smile as she waved her pink bouquet. Her hair was threaded with matching flowers, and her dress gleamed like a pearl. To Kenny, she was a princess.

Pride rose hot in his chest. His daughter. The most important thing in his life.

'You're beautiful!' he shouted, waving enthusiastically, forgetting about feeling foolish and Saturday shoppers. 'Absolutely gorgeous!'

Then he returned his hands to his pockets, conscious suddenly of the rest of the car's occupants. The other girls in bridesmaid get-up were Ed Wright's two. In the following hour they'd become Chloë's stepsisters.

And, in the centre, smiling awkwardly at him, was Shelly. He lifted his hand to her in a brief salute. She looked beautiful, too, but like a doll in a Cellophane box.

The lights changed and the car accelerated across the junction. He watched it disappear out of sight, Chloë's bouquet still flourishing in the back window.

Then he turned and strode back to number twenty-five, Bryant Street, a homely, red-brick terrace with a strip of flagstones for a front garden.

The street was jammed nose-to-tail with cars in front of dozens of houses similar to his.

After changing rapidly into his oldest jeans, Kenny returned to the street to work on his vehicle, pulled tight to the kerb, extracting his toolkit in its scuffed grey box from the boot and opening it on the pavement.

Blessed car. Mortifying that it should let him down this morning of all mornings he thought as he unlocked the car door, when he'd promised faithfully to get Chloë to Shelly in good time for the wedding.

He was a mechanic, for crying out loud! The skill in his two hands was sufficient to build a car from a handful of scrapped vehicles, which he had done, several times. It had shamed him to be beaten by an engine that refused to turn over.

He released the engine cover, muttering

under his breath to the pale blue car, its lovingly polished bright work winking in the sun.

'Really played me up, didn't you? Made me look a right twit.'

One good thing about Shelly getting married again was that Chloë was coming to stay with him while the newlyweds honeymooned.

Kenny loved having Chloë back in his home, occupying her old room, littering the place with her shoes or hair slides, her drawings lying around in unexpected places to bring him up short with their excellence.

Goodness knows where she'd come by her talent, but it certainly made him proud to look at her pictures.

Yesterday, she'd shown him a pen-and-ink drawing of the Old Manse that she was giving Shelly and Ed as a wedding present. Beautiful. He'd helped her choose a broad gilt frame for it, something they both thought went with the Old Manse's general air of elegance and permanence.

As he flipped open his socket set with a clatter, he thought of Shelly in the back of that Rolls, a stunning, expensively garbed bride, not looking anywhere near her thirty-five years.

The image of her on their own wedding day, despite it being sixteen years ago, was as clear to him as the vision of her today. And although they'd been apart for the last six, it was still strange to think of her stepping out of that Rolls Royce and walking up the broad steps of the town hall to marry another man.

For sixteen years she'd been Shelly Brannigan, and soon she'd become Shelly Wright.

She'd shrug off his name as if it were an outdated jacket and step into the lovely new life Ed Wright could give her.

He began to loosen the first spark plug.

Ed Wright owned a window factory. His vans were always buzzing about the town. *'Ave a new home with Avenue Windows!* was splashed in bold crimson letters on the sides. Ed himself always drove something brand new and flashy. Not for him an old but cherished Volkswagen Beetle, kept on the road by maintenance and willpower.

However glossy the paint and bright the chrome, a car like that didn't fit at the Old Manse, one of the largest of the Victorian palaces in the Avenue, kitted out with pretty much every modern luxury, Kenny didn't doubt.

Ed Wright could give Shelly and Chloë a

luxurious home full of pretty things, holidays and ... well, just about anything.

Kenny reached for his tools. The sun was warm on his back, and he began to relax, hands moving confidently over his equipment, the oily smell of an engine familiar and comforting.

He glanced at his watch. His girlfriend, Phillipa, would be arriving at lunchtime.

She'd dash along Broadway and into Bryant Street, her red-streaked hair flying, the costume jewellery she designed bright at her ears, neck and fingers.

She made the colourful, wacky jewellery to sell at local markets.

As she took a long lunch on Saturdays, because the two sixth-form girls she employed could man her stall, often Kenny would meet her among the red-brick buildings in town.

They'd eat baguettes in the sunshine at the crowded open-air market café, or slope off to the sweet-smelling coffee shop in the high street and drink espresso and eat chicken wraps. But not today.

'I'll nip along and cook us bacon and eggs,' she'd offered last night, kissing the corner of his mouth. 'Comfort food for if you're feeling down.'

Philly didn't need telling that he might feel emotional about Shelly remarrying. Philly didn't take a strop and turn jealous like a lot of women would, tearfully suspicious that he still harboured a passion for his former spouse. She understood that Shelly had left threads in the tapestry of his life.

And he didn't need to hide for her how strange it felt for Shelly to take Chloë to join another family. And the fact that the Wrights lived a life so far removed from his own only intensified the sensation that a gap was growing between himself and his daughter.

The service at the rather gothic town hall was soon over, but the photographs went on for ever, and the reception in the marquee on the lawns of the Old Manse went on even longer than that.

Speeches and toasts, the professionally served and artistically arranged food to go with the Pimms and champagne, oversized falls of pink or cream flowers overpowering the overheated marquee with their fragrance. Chloë's head had begun to throb as she sat alongside her mother at the top table.

She had to ignore her headache long enough to smile self-consciously when Ed made his speech, his top hat discarded but his cravat still beautifully tied and his tail-coat spotless.

'And I especially want to welcome Chloë to the family. And to say how delighted I am to have a new daughter.'

Chloë's thoughts flew to her dad, waiting on the corner this morning just to wave as she passed. How uncomfortable he'd looked in his best suit. His only suit. By now, she knew, he'd be back in his jeans, and probably with his hands black with oil.

She conjured up the way his brown eyes crinkled with love whenever she hugged him, thought of how he always had her favourite biscuits in the cupboard and her bed freshly made ready for the next time she'd stay.

And even though she retained the smile, a thought was revolving in her head.

I'm not Ed Wright's daughter. I'm Kenny Brannigan's.

The formalities concluded with the best man presenting the three bridesmaids with gleaming gold lockets. Melissa fastened hers immediately around her neck, Emily discarded hers carelessly in Melissa's bag, then the sisters jumped up to rush over to people they knew.

As Shelly had been borne away by Ed for

yet more photographs, Chloë was left at the table, clutching her locket in its smooth black box.

She'd said no more than hello to the other teenagers present. They belonged to Ed's cronies and were friends of Jason and Melissa, attending the same schools and pursuing the same interests.

She watched the laughing, chattering company for several minutes. Her mum was now pinned to Ed's side in the middle of a crush of men in suits wanting to shake Ed's hand and gallantly kiss the cheek of his bride.

Although she thought her mum looked stunning today, Chloë preferred her 'ordinary' look – natural and graceful, a slender figure in unfussy clothes.

The serving staff were beginning an efficient clear-up of the tables now. Chloë resisted the temptation to offer to help. Quietly, she slipped away from the table with its snowy cloth, the pink napkins bunched and tossed aside, and wandered out into the fresh air, leaving the hot, claustrophobic marquee behind in favour of the beautiful and tranquil gardens of the Old Manse.

Terraces stepped away from the house, and she wandered down over shelves of lush lawn and the stone steps that linked them. At the bottom she paused at the place where clematis rioted over a large archway in a close cut hedge to watch bees bumbling into the hearts of flowers like purple velvet saucers. Then she stepped through the arch.

The chatter and laughter of the wedding guests faded behind her.

This was her favourite part of Ed's garden. Here, behind the hedge, a massive pergola arched over a carp pond, creating welcome dappled shade and a cool, greenish serene atmosphere.

On this day when everything felt strange to her, the intruder – a feeling of unfamiliarity that never seemed to trouble Shelly - this nook of beauty would give her comfort.

An oak bridge arched over the pond, silver with age, and from there she gazed down at the koi carp, gold, silver, black, some as big as her arm, and the fish glided to the surface to gaze silently back. Their mouths moved all the time, as if they were muttering complaints.

She'd like to paint a picture of the pond, she thought, capture the lush greens and the flashes of colour. She was taking her GCSE next year, a year early, and there was a lot of coursework to be completed.

'Getting away from it all?'

Chloë whirled, almost losing her footing on the lichened planking in her satin shoes.

Jason was sitting on a black wrought-iron bench in the corner. He'd dumped his jacket and cravat, but still wore his striped trousers, white shirt and brocade waistcoat in the wedding colour scheme of dusky pink, cream and gold.

He looked apologetic.

'I made you jump,' he said. 'Sorry.'

She swallowed, heart still pattering.

'It's your garden.'

'Our garden.' He strolled over to join her on the bridge. His hair was a silken mop over his eyes and ears. She knew that Ed had wanted him to have it cut smarter, shorter, for the wedding, and Jason had politely resisted.

'Haven't you been listening to Dad?' He put on a loud and resolute voice, like Ed's. 'You're part of the family now, Chloë! The Old Manse is your home, just like it is for the rest of us.'

She grinned. Jason was nice, the best of her brand new step-family, friendly and comfortable to be with. She turned back to the fish, not wanting to make things awkward by pointing out that she'd been perfectly happy in the neat little house she'd shared with her mum, and even happier in the house where her dad still lived. This huge, eight-bedroom Victorian villa was a different world. A show home. A museum.

He laughed gently.

'Feels strange, doesn't it? Our parents marrying each other, making us all one big unit.' He shook fair hair out of grey eyes. 'I was just thinking about my mum. She used to love standing here to watch the fish.'

Chloë felt her insides shift with compassion. Annabelle, Ed's wife and the children's mother, had died several years ago.

The Old Manse had been her home, this garden hers. She might have planted the clematis that scrambled around the arch and the irises edging the pond, purple on one side of the water and yellow on the other. She'd probably chosen the fish, even the pearly white one, Chloë's favourite.

Her thoughts had been all for herself, and how strange she found everything; she hadn't considered the Wright children might feel strange, too.

'How do you feel about me and Mum invading your home?'

'How do you feel about moving into someone else's house?' he countered. 'It's definitely easier for us than you. We're happy that

Dad's happy again. And Shelly seems the kind who'll fit in without changing everything.'

Chloë didn't say that, by falling for Ed Wright, Shelly had certainly changed everything for her.

'So you really think that we're just going to slot right in without a problem?'

The sun reflected harshly from Jason's white shirt, and the breeze lifted his hair from his eyes. He turned to look at her thoughtfully.

'I think Melissa might find it hard to adjust,' he said delicately.

Chloë agreed. She was just relieved to hear Jason admit it.

Shelly smiled as she looked out of the window at the other cars they flashed past on the motorway. Their honeymoon had been magical.

It had been lovely to be alone, after all the organising of the wedding, her day in the spotlight. Lovely, too, to spend all day in shorts or sarongs, her hair hanging straight and unfettered past her shoulders.

Just how a honeymoon was meant to be. White beaches, turquoise sea, and that wonderful someone to stroll with hand-in-hand through the indigo dusk.

It didn't matter that now they were in the back of the car on the way home from the airport on a grey day, because her hand was still in Ed's, even though his other hand was occupied with a mobile phone as he talked to his children. It was taking him rather longer to chat to his four in turn than it had taken her to speak to her one.

Chloë had sounded fine, but Shelly couldn't wait to see her again. She wished the driver could transform the car into a helicopter and whizz over the traffic that suddenly seemed to be hemming them in.

However magical the honeymoon, she'd missed her daughter like mad, and felt her contentment would only be complete once she had Chloë beside her again.

Ed smiled and winked at her as he talked into the phone, and she beamed back. Since they married, Ed hadn't once asked Shelly if she was happy – he just seemed pretty confident that she was.

And he was right. Ed was a confident person. It was that and his air of authority that had first drawn her.

She hadn't been totally surprised to realise that the Ed she'd got to know on a historical society renovation project, with rust in his hair and green paint on his hands, with an obvious flair for organisation, was Edward Wright, local captain of industry.

But by then they'd shared several end-of-a-strenuous-day pizzas and a lot of laughter, and when he'd asked her out and turned up to fetch her in a car so new and fast that it shouted *MONEY!*, it didn't matter.

That they liked each other was what counted, and that his smile made her tummy flip, not what he had or what she didn't.

It was strange, of course it was, to be invited to a home that seemed palatial compared to her modern little semi, but it just so happened that he was a successful man. And, yes, she found him fresh and different.

Ed networked and made contacts at business breakfasts, he even had a 'coach' to make him question his own systems and strategies and see how they could be improved upon.

Goodness, he was different from easy-going, happy-where-he-was Kenny. Kenny, who would probably work at the same job in the same place all his life, and had never understood Shelly's drive for promotion.

She remembered his face when she came home one day and said she was going to take further qualifications, and it would mean three evenings a week at college.

'What for?' Kenny had been entirely baffled, his dark brown eyes staring at her without comprehension through equally dark hair that always needed cutting.

He'd barely understood her going back to work after Chloë was born. Going back to school as well was just beyond him.

'To move upwards.'

'Why?'

She'd struggled for a moment to reply to a question that, to her, didn't need asking.

'For more money, for instance!'

He'd looked around their little home.

'But we've got enough. We don't starve, do we? For goodness' sake, we've got two wages coming in! We can go to the cinema when we want, or the seaside. We've always got a car.'

She'd laughed, then.

'We've generally got two or three cars, Kenny, but whether any of them is whole and useable is another thing! OK, if we don't need more money, how about I do the course for the satisfaction, and the promotion to new and more interesting work that the qualification might bring me?'

That had thrown him. He'd stared at her and she'd known he was trying to grasp what she wanted and if it was something that he should have provided.

'Tell you what,' she'd temporised. 'You spend your weekends with your beloved cars, and I'll spend my evenings with my studying, and then we'll both be happy.'

It had seemed reasonable at the time, but, looking back on it, it was no wonder she and Kenny drifted apart. Equally, it was logical that, second time around, she'd chosen a different kind of man.

Ed snapped his phone shut.

'My lot are fine. How about Chloë?'

'Fine, too, of course – she's with her darling father!'

'But she's joining us today, isn't she? I'm looking forward to us all being together.' He bent to kiss her.

'Yes, darling. She's moved most of her stuff to your house–'

'Our house!'

'OK, our house! There are just the bigger items still to come, like her drawing board.'

'I'll send a van round.' He kissed her again gently and, as well as happy and tingly, Shelly felt very fortunate.

Kenny sat in his Volkswagen Beetle, Chloë beside him and Philly in the back seat, staring up the drive at the Old Manse. The

26

afternoon sun shone brightly through the windows of the car.

'It's time I went in,' Chloë said, making no move to do so.

Kenny patted her hand.

'I'll come to the door with you, to wish your mum and Ed well.' He didn't move, either.

Chloë smiled.

'It's nice that you and Mum are friendly when you meet. I hate rows.' Her hair hung in a glossy sheet, with the red earrings he'd bought her today from Philly's stall just peeping through her chestnut coloured hair.

He stroked a lock of it back behind her ears.

'Me, too!' He grinned, hoping his expression didn't look as stiff and unnatural as it felt.

'And Mum's got Ed. And you've got Philly.'

Kenny turned to wink at Philly, who sat in the back seat gazing up the drive.

'I don't think Philly thinks she's been "got".'

'I'm a free spirit, and one person can't own another,' Phillipa agreed automatically, gazing wide-eyed through the window. 'Is that all one house? Three storeys for just one family? Does each child get a suite of rooms?'

'Just one room each, but it leaves a few

spare.' Chloë meant the remark to be light-hearted, but it wasn't, somehow. The Old Manse didn't look any less daunting after a week in Kenny's house than it had at the wedding. Slowly, they climbed from the car, Kenny carrying Chloë's bag.

As they crunched up the drive, Shelly threw open the door and ran out to sweep Chloë into a hug. Her hair swung around her face, and she looked tanned and smart in white with touches of navy, and very happy.

Ed followed close behind, beaming his larger-than-life smile. He hugged Chloë, too, then shook hands enthusiastically with Kenny and Philly.

'You look very colourful today, Phillipa.'

Kenny glanced round at Philly as she smoothed down her turquoise velvet dungarees and tie-dyed amber T-shirt, the beads in her hair clashing cheerfully with the rest of her outfit.

'Yes, she looks great,' he declared. Philly always looked great; her clothes were a little wild and probably a bit clinging, but she was a happy, generous – and for that matter, pretty – woman. He felt uncertain. Was being colourful wrong? Had Ed meant it as a criticism?

An awkward pause seemed in danger of

developing. Kenny took Philly's hand and turned with a joviality he didn't feel to his ex-wife and her new husband.

'Well, all good luck for the future.'

'Thank you,' Shelly responded gravely.

'Won't you come in for a drink?' Ed gestured to the house's imposing front entrance. Kenny threw it a glance.

'Perhaps another time.' He kissed Chloë goodbye. 'Ring when you know which nights you want to come for your tea.'

She nodded.

'And I can go with you to the Great Billing car show next weekend, can't I?' She looked suddenly adrift; her big, blue eyes tugging at Kenny's heartstrings.

'You bet. Can't wait.' He hugged her fiercely, trying to convey with that one quick embrace how much he cared for her, that if she was unhappy, he'd make everything come right. Even if he didn't know how, yet. Then he nodded wordlessly to Shelly and Ed and turned away, towing Philly behind, hurrying, faster, faster.

It felt as if his heart had moved up to the back of his throat, choking him, making his eyes sting and burn.

Six years ago, when Shelly had gone her own way, taking Chloë with her, he'd thought he'd known what heartache was. That dull, physical need in his chest, that hollow missing-you that cloaked the universe in grey drizzle.

But he'd just discovered it was nothing compared to watching his daughter step into her new world.

Living at the Old Manse was going to be like living in a hotel, Chloë suspected.

'Wear something nice for dinner, darling, won't you?' her mother had whispered. So Chloë dressed in a new floaty top from the market, with her favourite black trousers.

They all sat down together at a large round table that Chloë already knew could be made a larger oval if required.

'A celebratory dinner,' Ed declared.

Chloë wondered just how many celebrations they were going to have. Over the last few months they'd had the engagement, a setting-the-date dinner, a welcoming Shelly and Chloë supper, and a pre-wedding lunch. And there was always a snowy white tablecloth. Chloë had been used to eating at the kitchen table when it was just her and Shelly, and that didn't need a cloth because you could just wipe it over after every meal.

But dinner was delicious. Barbara, the

daily help, had left the table set prettily with silver cutlery and yellow and white flowers, and all Shelly had to do was take the chicken casserole out of the oven when the new potatoes had been cooked in the microwave. No-one washed their dirty dishes when they'd finished. They just abandoned them by the sink for Barbara to stack in the dishwasher in the morning. It seemed no-one bothered with mundane tasks, because Ed also employed a gardener twice a week. Very odd, to Chloë.

They all moved into the sitting-room where Shelly poured the coffee, looking self-conscious as she handled the pretty, flower-festooned china.

Ed laughed and joked with his children. These few minutes to relax together after a meal seemed a pleasant daily custom. Melissa, eyes shining, was full of news about people that Chloë knew only vaguely or not at all, Jason contributed few words but smiled a lot. Emily talked about her beloved pony, Junk, and Patrick told pointless, eight-year-old's jokes – loudly.

Ed, however, seemed keen to include his new stepdaughter.

'Tell us all what you've been doing this week, Chloë.'

Chloë had been quite content to listen without contributing. She shifted on the tan, ultra-squashy sofa.

'I went with Dad to an autojumble – he found some parts for another car he's rebuilding. Philly came, too. She says Dad's a car maniac, not a car mechanic.

'She calls the car a "Corset", but it's a Corsair. He took down the fence so he could get the car in the back garden, and he hasn't put it back yet.'

She laughed. Then stopped. The politely blank faces suggested that probably only Shelly had the remotest idea what an autojumble was or why anyone should care about the Corsair.

Shelly smiled encouragingly.

'I remember plenty of wet weekends spent trudging around stalls and stalls of second-hand car parts.'

The polite gazes remained fixed on Chloë, obviously assuming she'd done more than visit one autojumble in a week.

'I finished the design for the cover for our class Art project,' she stumbled on, hoping this, at least, was something they'd have an understanding of.

'And I've got an appointment to see Ms Meredith about my Art coursework. And

I'm doing a painting of Dad's Beetle. For his birthday.'

'He'll love that,' Shelly put in. 'Anything to do with his old cars!'

Chloë smiled gratefully at her, even if she thought her mum could be a little less obvious with her heartening remarks.

Ed smiled widely.

'Well, Chloë, we want to get you settled in as soon as possible. I intend to get your drawing board brought here tomorrow.'

'Oh. Thanks.' Chloë juggled her cup and saucer, thinking about one of Ed's swanky sign-written vans turning up at their old house, the *For Sale* board standing in the garden.

'Where's the best place for this drawing board, do you think?'

Chloë hesitated. She wished Ed didn't have to make quite such a show of being kind to her. It made her feel conspicuous and uncomfortable.

'In my room?' She stuttered annoyingly over the word 'my'.

'Hmm.' Ed stroked his chin, then winked an exaggerated wink at Shelly. 'Actually, your mother and I were thinking that you might like to use the big room over the garage for your drawing and painting. It could be your studio. There's a door to it near your bedroom, at the end of the landing. It's empty at the moment and there are skylights–'

'But you wouldn't let me have that room when I wanted to make it into a gym!' Melissa burst out.

Ed turned his attention to his daughter.

'I wouldn't spend thousands of pounds buying equipment that you'd probably only use twice,' he corrected mildly.

His frown and the reproof in the gaze he fixed on Melissa made Chloë suspect that he was more annoyed than his tone suggested. She felt a wriggle of worry as her heart sank.

Melissa's voice tightened, and her face went first red, and then white.

'But why should she have that room just because she can draw a bit? You said you wanted to make her feel welcome, not treat her like a child star!'

'Don't stress, Mel,' Jason interposed gently.

Chloë threw a worried look at her mum. Shelly was biting her lip and staring at this strange, glittery-eyed Melissa.

'That's enough!' Ed didn't raise his voice, but sounded pretty decisive for all that. 'Melissa, act your age.'

Melissa glared, then whirled as if to leave the room.

'Sit down! Please.'

After a moment, Melissa sat, blinking hard, in mutinous silence.

Chloë stared down again at her cup. She hadn't drunk any of the coffee and felt that her thumping heart would rise up to choke her if she tried. She cleared her throat.

'I don't need a special room. The drawing board will fit in my bedroom. There's loads of space.'

Her quiet voice seemed not to be heard.

Ed's attention was still on his daughter.

'Melissa, I'm sure you didn't mean to sound so unwelcoming towards Chloë. You'll remember that I told you Chloë won't be treated any differently to the rest of you; she's part of our family now. She'll be able to go to school at St Paul's, like you and Emily, in the new academic year.'

'What?' It was Chloë's turn to blanch.

'And I'll provide whatever's necessary for her to cultivate her special interests and gifts, in just the same way that I got the paddock for Emily, and the pony. And just like I bought you a saxophone and clarinet you hardly ever play, Melissa! If I think it's best for Chloë to have a studio, she will have one.'

35

Chloë tried again.

'I don't want one!'

'I don't see why she needs a studio.' Melissa had managed to modify her tone, but her cheeks were flushed again with anger.

Shelly interrupted worriedly.

'Perhaps we could discuss it later, Ed.'

Chloë turned to Ed, who looked as if he didn't know whether to be dumbfounded or angry.

'You're trying to be very kind. But I don't want to pretend that you're my dad.'

'We all understand that,' Jason began.

'I don't think so,' Chloë declared. 'Or Ed wouldn't be trying to decide everything for me and act as if I've always lived here and know everyone you all know! As if, if he does a good enough job on me no-one will realise I'm an addition. It's like covering two different lots of chairs with the same fabric and then insisting they're a suite. But I'm me! I'm still me! And I don't want to pretend I'm not!'

Chapter Two

'So will it be all right if he comes with us?' Chloë pressed the telephone to her ear, knowing from the deep pause on the other end of the line that, as she'd anticipated, her father wasn't enthusiastic.

'What's he want to come for? I never knew he liked car shows. It's only a tiddly little show, too, not a big posh one. He doesn't think it's going to be full of shiny vintage Bentleys, does he?' Kenny sounded every bit as dubious as Chloë had feared.

'I don't think so. I think he's just ... being friendly.' She gazed out of the window over the gardens that stepped away from the big house. Barbara, the Wright family's daily help, was bringing in washing from the line at the very bottom of the long terraced garden. Fresh white washing, perfect, like an advert for washing powder. 'Jason's nice, Dad.'

'Well ... if you'd like him to come, I suppose it'll be OK.' Kenny still sounded baffled. 'But I don't know what we'll have to say to each other, it's not that we'd have anything in common.' He paused, then added, judiciously, 'Still, he's part of your new family, so if he'd really like to be with us you'd better tell him to be ready on Saturday morning.'

When the call was over Chloë picked up her pad and flopped onto the pretty yellow cotton that covered the thick duvet on her bed, gazing down at the rough drawing of a tiger that she was working on. She knew her father would rather that Chloë's new stepbrother, Jason, didn't impinge on their precious time together, and, to be truthful, Chloë wondered about it herself. But she was all too well aware that Jason had been trying to help her out of a difficult situation by suggesting it.

She sighed, studying her page with dissatisfaction. Drawing tigers was not nearly as easy as you'd think. The folds of flesh hanging down from their bellies made them look very odd on paper, a bit boat-like and tubby. Chewing the end of her pencil she tried to think of ways to give the impression of the slinky movement of a Sumatran Tiger.

Instead, she found herself going over for the tenth time the irritating exchange at breakfast that morning. Melissa, sipping black coffee and picked delicately at a small bowl of cereal in a beam of sunlight coming in through the tall window that looked out towards The Avenue, had amused herself by bombarding Chloë with questions about her father's fascination with old cars. It was the older girl's languidly patronising tone that had made Chloë feel defensive, rather than the actual questions – which were unexceptional enough.

'But what *happens* at a car show? Do the cars race around a track?'

Chloë had at first remained patient. 'No, that would be a race meeting. The cars are just … on show.'

'What, do you mean just to *look* at?' Melissa had made this sound the feeblest occupation imaginable as she fiddled with the length of her smooth brown hair. 'And what else is there at a car show?' She stirred her cereal idly, her eyebrows raised in exaggerated interest.

Chloë began to stumble slightly. 'There are stalls, you know, the autojumble.'

'Autojumble.' Melissa drew the word out consideringly. 'Remind me?'

Cheeks pinkening, Chloë returned with a snap, 'It's where people buy and sell their second-hand car parts. Shall I explain what second-hand means, too? I don't suppose your father's ever bought you anything that's not sparkling new!' She stared at her stepsister, face burning. It was as well that Shelly had already left the table to get ready for work, because Chloë was well aware that her mother would have had something to say about Chloë unsheathing her claws like that.

And Melissa's eyes narrowed angrily as she opened her mouth to retort.

But that had been Jason's cue to join the conversation, smoothly and calmly diffusing the situation with his calm friendliness. 'Sounds great, Chloë! I'm really keen on cars at the moment, can't wait to take my test in a couple of weeks. I don't suppose I could come along this weekend, could I? Do you think your dad would mind?'

With an effort, Chloë shifted her angry gaze from Melissa and recalled her manners. 'You'll be very welcome, I'm sure,' she managed. 'I'll ring Dad about it later.'

While Melissa snatched up her blazer and stalked out to wait for the coach that took her to her school, Chloë collected dishes, annoyed that she'd let Melissa nettle her.

Jason had slanted her a complicit smile from behind his long fringe. 'Maybe we should invite Mel?'

With a giggle, Chloë cheered up, glad that

Jason, at least, had a way to manage his sister.

Dragging the book on endangered species closer to her across the bed she thought about car shows and how they'd appear to an outsider. The shows had a relaxed atmosphere as the interested and the expert subjected rows of polished vehicles to slow scrutiny and constantly swapped anecdotes and information. She loved the vague tang of oil mingling on the air with the appetising smell of burgers from the van, the glow of lovingly polished paintwork, the bright gleam of chrome in the sun. It had been part of her world for as long as she could remember. But she supposed that it might seem a strange way of spending a Saturday to some!

No need for Melissa to be so superior about it, though.

She sighed, and tried again to concentrate on the way a tiger's stripes lay over his shoulder muscles.

After an intense day with a difficult to please client, Shelly parked her car in the drive of The Old Manse, looking forward to the relief of changing out of her suit. Pausing to breathe in a balmy early spring evening and fill her senses with the honeysuckle that was a pink and yellow froth nearby, she let her shoulders relax on the out breath as she'd been taught in yoga classes in the days when she'd had time to attend them.

That seemed a while back, she thought, back before she'd steered her Information Technology experience into the fast-paced world of marketing. Now she was a consultant with a big agency, liaising with clients on their Internet requirements and then with the agency's web-design team to make certain that they correctly interpreted the clients' needs. It was her aim to ensure that the clients were so happy that they would never go anywhere else. It meant that she now had to commute to the London office a couple of times a week, which could be exhausting. But it was worth it. She *loved* her job.

She gazed up at the house as she locked the pretty new scarlet hatchback that had been waiting for her on her return from honeymoon, acknowledging how quickly she'd learnt to enjoy coming 'home' to this stalwart Victorian building with its big sliding sash windows and tall chimneys.

Ed was waiting for her in the comfortable sitting room looking relaxed in a dark blue short-sleeved shirt that brought out the colour of his eyes.

She dropped her handbag on a chair and shrugged out of her jacket before planting a kiss on his lips and dropping down beside him on the sofa. 'Have you been home long?'

He gave her his wide smile as he dropped the paper in order to take her hand. 'I finished a bit early, I thought we'd go out to dinner. I've booked a table at that bistro you like – The Grape Vine.'

Shelly was slightly ashamed to feel her heart dip. 'Go out? But what about the children?'

He winked. 'All arranged! Jason has agreed to stay in with Patrick and Emily, the others can look after themselves, can't they? Barbara has left pie and potatoes in the oven and I'm sure Jason or Melissa can manage a few peas. A nice evening alone seemed just the ticket! And I've even left you time to get ready. We're not due there for an hour.'

Resigning herself to the fact that there wasn't going to be an evening on the couch as she climbed to her feet, Shelly went first to check that Chloë was happy with Ed's arrangements.

Chloë simply flashed one of her beaming smiles. 'I've phoned Dad and arranged an extra evening with him and Philly, that's OK, isn't it?'

'Of course, darling.' Shelly dropped a kiss on her daughter's cheek then left her to finish studding her long hair with beaded ornaments from Philly's stall ready for when Kenny arrived to pick her up, probably in the elderly blue Beetle. A vision popped suddenly into her mind of a much younger Kenny coming to pick Shelly up, before they were even married, in a bright red Isetta 'Bubble Car'. She remembered the laughter as he'd proudly showed her his newest acquisition, the tiny car that he insisted fit his pocket, nicknamed the 'The Rolling Egg' by their friends.

Underpowered and cramped, it had still been tons of fun.

She remembered for a moment when everything for the youthful Kenny and Shelly had been fun.

Taking a few minutes to shower, she dressed in a fresh outfit, scolding herself that she was becoming spoilt. A year ago she would have been excited and delighted, no matter how fatigued she was, to be asked – taken – to the plush environs of The Grape Vine. A year ago it would have meant rushing home from work to prepare a meal for Chloë, throwing washing in the machine and putting together sandwiches for the next day, before

44

getting herself ready at the speed of light.

But now that she'd adopted Ed's comfortable lifestyle, coming home to find she had only to add the finishing touches to a delicious meal that Barbara had left, safe in the knowledge that the housework and laundry were the responsibility of somebody else, it seemed almost a chore to get ready to go out to dinner!

How easily she'd accustomed herself to the good life!

She grinned at herself in the mirror, opened the wardrobe and chose a dress, a denim blue one that she hadn't worn before.

Once she was sitting at a table with a burgundy red linen cloth set with shiny silverware and gleaming glasses she was glad she'd made the effort, enjoying the appetising fragrances of garlic and roasting vegetables wafting from the kitchens. Ed was his usual attentive self. Nothing was ever too much trouble for him, he always took pains to make certain that Shelly had everything she wanted and was assured but pleasant with the restaurant staff.

Relaxed, she began to chatter about the work of which she was so proud. 'I'm being pulled out of the local office more and more often and given larger and more prestigious clients, inevitably many of them are based in London.'

She broke off to allow Ed to order, salad for her, pasta for him.

'That means travel, of course,' she went on, 'which means longer hours. And I was quite footsore by the time I got home tonight because I was too late to get a seat on the train.'

Ed broke a breadstick. 'If it's too much, darling, perhaps it's time you left the agency altogether and joined the business? Then there would be no more late evenings.'

Wineglass frozen on its way to her mouth Shelly stared at her new husband as he flicked away with an air of unconcern the crumbs he'd just made. His words had to click through her mind at least twice before she was certain she'd understood him correctly.

'Work *for you*, do you mean?'

He smiled, leaning back to allow the waiter to place a bottle of sparkling water on the table. 'I wouldn't call it working *for* me, darling, as we're married! But I can't deny that I'd like you to give *our* business all that expertise you have, move us forward in the technological stakes.'

Shelly poured a glass of water to give herself time to think, the bottle very cold in her hand. As the sparkling clear liquid trickled she passed under review the systems in place at the offices of Avenue Windows.

Standard accounting packages and estimating and design programmes was all she could come up with. How could she occupy herself all day with those?

She felt incredulous, almost angry at such airy but wildly inaccurate pigeonholing. There was nothing there to challenge her, utilise her skills, advance her career, or provide any sign of job satisfaction at all! In fact, just the thought of being shut away in those offices was sufficient to make her feel bored and claustrophobic.

'It's not my area,' she pointed out carefully, through suddenly stiff lips. 'I don't understand where you see me fitting in.'

Ed looked nonplussed. Shelly's Caesar salad and Ed's hearty plate of pasta with a chicken and tomato sauce arrived. The clatter and chatter of the restaurant ebbed and flowed around them as Shelly waited for Ed to speak.

'I was thinking you could take over the Information Technology side. You've just said you aren't happy with commuting and dealing with large clients.'

She shook her head, decisively, once, working hard on staying calm. 'I didn't say that I wasn't happy with it! I just said I did it.'

Ed took her hand. 'But you don't need to, don't need to try so hard, now that we're married. I realise you won't want to give up work altogether but it would be appropriate to downshift a bit, don't you think?' He loaded his fork with pasta and creamy sauce.

'Appropriate?' Despite her best intentions Shelly felt her temper begin to balloon at his easy dismissal of everything she'd worked so hard for. All those years of night school and course work and exams at the end of days already full to bursting with a full-time job and caring for her darling daughter. All the careful preparation for job interviews! Suddenly she found herself leaning forward, regarding him fiercely across the Chianti. 'Do you have *any* idea of what I actually do?'

Ed slowly became still.

Shelly went on. 'I deal with ideas and concepts, campaigns and market management. I'm not a "techie" who keeps your systems running and analyses your requirements. That, and what *I* do, having nothing in common other than the actual use of a computer! It's like–' She hunted around for an illustration he'd relate to. 'It's like you asking your window fitters to put a new roof on a house just because both jobs require a ladder!'

A silence followed her words, a silence that seemed to ring around the restaurant. Shelly was shocked to realise that the clink of cutlery had halted, that people were gazing her way. She flushed to think she'd spoken vehemently enough to disturb others from their meals.

'I see.' Ed's voice was extra quiet, as if to emphasise how loud her words had been. He met her gaze, unsmiling, then turned deliberately to his food.

Shelly's appetite had fled. She laid her fork aside with the lovely meal barely touched.

Her heart banged in her chest.

He was angry with her.

She was angry with him, too, but she shouldn't have embarrassed him by making the entire restaurant aware of her displeasure. She wished that she'd dealt with his off-beam suggestion a little more thoughtfully. Smiled perhaps and said lightly but with finality that she was fine as she was. There had been no need for her to be so sharply emphatic, so scornful.

But just for a moment she'd been furious at Ed's attitude that he was offering her a marvellous opportunity when, in fact, he was diminishing her skills in suggesting something so far out of her experience and at a comparatively small company with no opportunity for advancement.

Was he trying to pull her into line, to put her into a little box so that he could oversee her? Who was he to take the decision for her to 'downshift'? Was this how Chloë had felt when Ed tried to organise her workroom and change her school, this outrage that he should overstep the boundaries that separated individuals and disregard the will of another?

She breathed deeply, gathering her thoughts. At the bottom of her she knew that Ed didn't mean to take charge, but it would be all too easy to become subsumed by his strong personality, to be made a part of his life instead of having a life of her own. Perhaps the attributes that had made him attractive originally now seemed to have a possibly different and less palatable slant: controlling rather than confident and bossy instead of authoritative.

But then she looked at the hurt bafflement on his face as he picked silently at his food. Ed genuinely wanted what was best for Shelly.

Dismayingly, he thought it was up to him to make it happen.

Having reacted so strongly, it was now up to her to dissipate the crackle of anger in the air. So she covered his hand with hers and said what she should have said in the first place. 'You don't have to worry about me, darling. I'm very happy where I am, thank you.'

'Fine.' Ed continued to eat, without expression.

'I'm sorry,' she said, more quietly. 'You touched an old wound. All I ever had from Kenny was that I should stay home more and forget my ambitions. Why did I have to be so driven to advance, why couldn't I just be content and count my blessings? That's why things didn't work out between us, I'm afraid. He didn't allow me to be myself.'

By the time Saturday morning came around, Chloë had become used to the idea of Jason going along to the car show. As it was such a lovely morning they walked down to Kenny's house out of The Avenue and through the geometric streets of houses. Around them, people washed their cars or walked their dogs in the sunshine and she felt her heart lift at the prospect of the familiar, good-natured atmosphere of a car show.

Her dad hadn't been enthusiastic about Jason joining them but Jason, wearing jeans, T-shirt and trainers, as she was, looked as if he'd fit right in. A small silver camera hung from his belt.

They reached Bryant Street in time to climb into the cramped back seat of Kenny's pale blue Volkswagen Beetle, obviously freshly washed. Jason endeared himself to Kenny immediately. 'Wow, cool car!'

Chloë watched her father's chin lift in pride. '1977, 1.6 air-cooled engine. Been round the clock twice, rebuilt the engine myself and restored her bodywork.'

'Wow,' Jason repeated. 'She's brilliant.'

From the front seat, Philly sighed, twisting around to grin at Chloë. 'Suppose he's going to talk cars all day, now! Young Jason's a fresh audience for him.'

Chloë grinned back. She would be perfectly happy for Kenny to bend Jason's ear all day – much better than them not knowing what to say to one another. Not that there was much sign of it at the moment.

'I'm taking driving lessons,' Jason was telling Kenny eagerly. 'My test's in a couple of weeks, I've already passed my theory. I've got the money for a car, I've been saving up my pay from working at Dad's place in the holidays.' His eyes shone with enthusiasm.

'Must be handy having a dad like that,' Kenny observed dryly, checking his mirrors, indicating and pulling away from the kerb.

Jason laughed. 'I don't get special treatment for being the boss's son, if that's what you're implying. I get sent out on the vans with the skilled men and spend all day carrying windows and holding ladders and fetching tools! I sometimes think they give me the heaviest end of everything on principle.'

Kenny nodded in approbation. 'That's the best way to do it. Learn from the bottom. Won't do you any harm.'

'I suppose not. I'd rather be doing something to do with engines, but I couldn't find a garage that would take me on just during the holidays.'

'No, well they'll all want lads who can commit to training,' Kenny agreed. 'Although I'll ask at our place for the summer holidays, if you want?'

'Cool!' agreed Jason. 'That would be brilliant!'

The showground, Billing Aquadrome, a country park with a lake and caravans, was filling up by the time they reached it. Kenny wasn't exhibiting but so many enthusiasts like him attended that the car park held almost as many older vehicles as the show area.

He and Jason fell in together to peruse the ranks of shining, cherished vehicles of all makes and some of very modest origins, Kenny pointing out various features as he talked, Jason listening intently in between taking photos. Chloë and Philly soon left them to their admiration of gleaming chrome and candy-coloured paintwork, moved on to a few stalls that held key-rings and T-shirts, and finally found the tea stand with its wooden benches and tables around it on the trodden grass.

'Lovely weather.' Philly turned her face up to the late spring sun. Her cinnamon singlet over a cherry red T-shirt was a striking combination. Amber glass beads fell in long strands from her earlobes. 'I adore hot weather. I'd love to live in a hot country. You know, I always intended to travel more than I have.'

'Did you? Yes, you being a free spirit you'd take to travelling like a duck to water.' Chloë grinned, seeing in her mind's eye Philly tramping the streets of the world with a rucksack and a compass. 'Where do you fancy? Australia? Egypt? Japan? China?'

Philly didn't smile. She threw back her

hair and looked earnest and wistful instead. *'All* of those! Can you imagine? Sydney Harbour, The Tokyo Tower, the pyramids, the Great Wall of China? Seeing those things for yourself? Mixing with the people whose country it is? Absorbing their culture, eating their food, wearing the same clothes...'

Chloë wasn't certain that she would like to embrace a different culture quite so closely, but then she'd never even been out of her own country. But, 'Sounds brilliant,' she agreed, because Philly's rapt expression evinced such enthusiasm that she would've felt mean voicing her own misgivings.

Philly gazed up into the deep blue of the sky. 'Perhaps I ought to get on with it instead of spending my whole life just talking about it.' And suddenly the look on her face was one of determination.

As if the wind had turned, Chloë felt a chill creep over her body. Philly was serious. Did she intend Kenny to go with her? Chloë wanted to ask, but the words were thick and reluctant to move over her tongue.

Philly sighed. 'It would be just perfect. Just for a year or two I mean, not forever.'

Chloë thought about a year not seeing her father, and the sun went in on the rest of the day.

55

She was quiet on the way home, unable to match Jason's enthusiasm for the show.

'I'd *love* something like that,' he kept saying, flicking his long hair back from his face. 'Wouldn't it be cool to whizz around town in a car that's older than I am? I *love* those Ford Anglias! That back window's too crazy for words. I liked that one with the metal dashboard. Did you see it, Chloë? Wicked, wasn't it?'

'Wicked,' Chloë agreed, hardly hearing his words.

Calm and clear spring evenings deserved to be enjoyed, Kenny felt. He was boxed up all day inside the garage where he worked, now there was a bit of light of an evening he liked to find some reason to be out in it when it was fine. His arm moved in a slow, contemplative circling as he applied a fresh coat of polish to the roof of the Beetle.

Automatically, he looked up as the lazy, mellow grumbling of a powerful engine in low gear rumbled up the street.

Then he paused.

He had to make his arm resume the methodical polishing as the expensive modern car slid into a parking space and Ed Wright locked it before crossing to where

Kenny worked. Ed stepped onto the pavement, shirt neat, hair brushed. 'This is the pride and joy then, eh?'

'One of them.' Carefully Kenny tipped the bottle of liquid wax against the cloth and moved on to a new section of the roof spreading the liquid evenly.

Ed shuffled, and slid his hands into his pockets. He wore tailored trousers, not jeans. 'Kind of you to take young Jason out last week.'

Kenny frowned at a tiny blemish in the paintwork, rubbing it carefully with one fingertip. He'd have to watch that in case it bubbled up into a rust spot. 'He told my Chloë he'd like to come to the show. Good lad he is. No trouble.'

'A good lad, yes.' Ed laughed. 'Typical teenager, though. Full of wild ideas.'

Looking up at the sky, Kenny judged that the light was failing fast. He picked up a clean cloth to take the polish off. He wondered what Ed wanted and hoped it wouldn't take long. Or else he'd find himself having to invite Ed in. He didn't fancy that at all, Ed standing in his small sitting room with the elderly flecked carpet and comfortable but equally elderly suite and comparing it to his big house. But he could scarcely stand out here in the darkness, could he? 'Seems a sensible type to me,' he observed, mildly.

Ed sighed. 'He's got some extraordinary idea about buying a classic car, though, when he passes his test. I told him it was out of the question, of course.'

Kenny didn't answer, but shook out his cloth in search of a clean place.

'He'd be buying a packet of trouble.' Ed ran his fingertip absently along the chrome strip around the car's windscreen. 'I told him that. He's got enough money to buy something only a few years old. And I'd help him if he was being sensible. He knows that. He could have a nice little runaround.'

Ah. That was the purpose of Ed's visit. He was looking for Kenny to scotch Jason's enthusiasm for buying a 30-year-old car. Kenny wiped his hands on his jeans and dropped his cloth into his kit box. The polish, lid carefully tightened, followed. 'I have told him about the disadvantages. You have to have a bit of time to devote to the older vehicle.'

Ed's head swung up eagerly. 'Have you? I hope he sees it's a stupid idea, then!'

Slowly, Kenny turned and looked at the other man, all neat and smart. He wasn't warm and friendly like young Jason. 'I'm not so sure it's a *stupid idea*. He'd get a lot of fun out of a car like that. Taking bits apart, making it work. Especially now he's got that summer job at our garage.'

Instantly, he cursed himself as Ed's face reflected dismay.

'Summer job at *your* garage?'

'The garage where I work,' Kenny corrected, shutting the lid of the kit box down tightly.

'But he has a holiday job with my company!' Ed looked bewildered.

Kenny shrugged. 'He asked me to ask about jobs, and there's a young lad got to have three months off for an operation, so they've offered it to your lad. Bit of a grease monkey, you know. Learn from the bottom.' And then, uneasy in the sort of tense silence that made him wonder whether Ed was about to explode, added, 'All experience for him, isn't it?'

'Of a type,' sighed Ed, digging out his car keys from his trouser pocket.

'I shouldn't worry too much,' Kenny said impulsively, just as Ed swung away. 'I don't think the car idea will come off.'

Slowly, Ed turned back. In the dusk, his face was all in shadow.

'The insurance companies will refuse to

quote,' Kenny explained succinctly. 'Don't think they'll wear a youngster like that driving a car where the parts aren't readily available. I told him, suggested he ring up and find out. Better he discovers the realities of owning a car himself, rather than me telling him. But I think he'll be disappointed.'

'He didn't tell me anything about the insurance,' Ed said, tightly. 'He's got a silly habit sometimes of withholding information from me almost for the sake of it.' Then he seemed to relax. 'Still. Good thing if it stops him getting lumbered with some old heap.'

Kenny passed his hand gently over the curving lines of his beloved car, giving himself a second to get over a flash of irritation. 'It must be difficult when they get to eighteen and have to be left to make their own decisions and their own mistakes. But I wouldn't let him buy a heap. I would've looked after him.'

'Of course you would! Of course!' In his embarrassment Ed became bluff and hearty. 'Just as I look after Chloë.'

For a second Kenny felt the irritation explode into an emotion that he never remembered experiencing before. It wasn't anger; it was some nameless passion, a protest against anyone taking even an atom of his paternal role away from him. Blood filled his head, throbbing and pulsing in his temples and at the sides of his neck. But all he said was, 'Chloë's already got two parents. Her mother's done a wonderful job of bringing her up.'

Looking startled, Ed stepped back. 'Of course! I didn't mean...'

Kenny made himself relax. 'Difficult, isn't it, when your child comes under the influence of someone else?'

And that makes us even, Mr Wright, Kenny thought, as the powerful car purred off into the night. Ed had been none to shy about showing he didn't really like Jason being friendly with Kenny, moving in Kenny's alien world of things that weren't new and shiny. And now Ed knew that Kenny wasn't terribly keen at Ed having a say in Chloë's life.

Ever since Shelly married again, Kenny's stomach had been shrinking at the thought of all the lovely things that Ed Wright could bestow upon Kenny's daughter, the wonderful life he could afford to give her. The holidays and the clothes and the private education.

Yet here was Ed himself, just as uneasy because Jason wanted to buy an old car like Kenny's.

'What are you doing out here in the dark?'

Chloë looked up. She'd heard Jason's whistle as he strode down the lawns to the carp pond behind the hedge, so his appearance hadn't startled her. 'What are *you* doing out here in the dark?' she countered.

He laughed. 'I come here when I want a bit of peace.'

She got to her feet. 'I'll go back to the house—'

'No you won't.' He pulled her down with him as he flopped down onto the bench. Jason did everything in fluid, unhurried motions; he slouched when he stood, gangled when he walked, lounged when he sat down. He was tall and whippy, like a greyhound. 'I don't mind sharing the dark garden with you. You're not indescribably noisy like Emily and Patrick, and you're not ratty and superior like Mel. You can stay.'

She giggled at his mock condescending manner, but settled again on the hard slats of the old bench.

'I do like your dad, Chloë,' he went on. 'He knows such a lot about motors! All the makes and models, and how to keep them in mint condition. He knows loads of people and the types of cars they're interested in. And he's funny, too, isn't he? Very dry humoured.'

Chloë swallowed. 'Yes. He's good with cars.'

'So,' said Jason. 'What are you out here worrying about?'

In the darkness, she felt her face flush. But she didn't want to discuss the horrible squirmy feeling she'd nursed since Philly had expressed an interest in travelling. If Kenny went with Philly, perhaps they'd buy an old camper van to travel across the continents in. She could see that they'd love that kind of life. Living like gypsies, taking work where they could find it. 'Not much,' she fibbed. 'I just wanted to be quiet. How about you?'

Jason let out a groan, and thumped the bench beside him. 'I can't get an insurance company to insure me for a classic car. Got to be at least twenty-one, apparently.' The second sigh was still bigger.

Chloë tutted sympathetically. 'Oh no! Well, I suppose you'll just have to wait then. You can get a modern car for now. Your dad will be pleased, at least.'

Jason ran a fingernail gloomily along the ribbed side of his trainers. 'Hmm. He ought to be. The trouble is....' He scraped his nail on the rubber ribbing more and more quickly. It made a noise like a big grasshopper chirruping in the purple evening.

'Trouble is that I've already agreed to buy one.'

Chapter Three

Jason looked up from his orange juice as Chloë whirled into the sun-filled kitchen and looped her black school sweatshirt onto the back of a chair. Then she placed some sheets of paper carefully on the seat to keep them flat.

It wasn't unusual to see Chloë with a card folder protecting her precious painting and drawings, of course.

'Important stuff?' He poured orange juice for himself and Patrick, who was taking advantage of his father's absence from the breakfast table to read at the table. It was safer to pour for him; it saved mopping up time in the long run. Jason noticed that Melissa had seated herself carefully across the table from their younger brother, as if that excused her from keeping an eye on him.

Chloë rolled her eyes. 'I've got a before-school meeting with Mrs Meredith today to hand in my coursework and have a "one-to-one". Mrs Meredith's famous for her one-to-ones. She always begins with, "Let's see where we are, shall we?" and then she tells you where *she* thinks you are. And it's usually several levels below where *you* think you are! You end up promising her fresh energy and effort, and, *especially,* that you will go to sleep at night contemplating the utmost importance of GCSE Art coursework.

'"Coursework, coursework, coursework ... concentrate on your coursework ... keep up to date ... consistently produce your very best..."' Chloë flopped into a chair, shook cereal into a bowl, added milk, and took two croissants to go with it.

Jason grinned. 'Hungry?'

'If I've got to cope with Mrs Meredith's attention first thing in the morning, I need a good breakfast,' she said, solemnly, although her eyes were dancing.

'Wozzat?' asked Patrick, indistinctly, raising his eyes from a lurid comic to pay attention to the conversation, his mouth occupied with toast and jam.

'My art coursework. I have to get it in today.'

'C'nav a yook?' Patrick chewed and swallowed. 'Can I have a look, please?'

Chloë pulled the chair around. 'You're welcome to look, but don't touch with those jammy fingers! I had a lot of trouble getting it right.' She opened the folder and spread the pages out for his inspection.

'Mega cool.' Patrick pulled his face into an exaggerated expression of approval, eyebrows up and cheeks ballooned. Then he reached for another piece of toast.

Jason joked gently, 'Wow! You've achieved something if you've impressed Patrick.'

Melissa craned across to take a look. 'The artist's opus. Shouldn't it be under armed guard or something?'

Chloë seemed prepared to take this as a joke. She glanced about herself in an exaggeratedly furtive manner, whispering, 'Why? Who do you think might do something to it?'

The other girl shrugged, and reached simultaneously for the coffee pot and the morning newspaper, becoming instantly absorbed in the front page. With a keen interest in current affairs, Melissa had a way of doing this whenever she got hold of the daily paper or watched the news on television, tuning out everyone around her.

Jason watched Chloë slant an assessing look at Melissa before shrugging and turning her attention to her cereal.

He wished away this tension between his sister and his new stepsister. Melissa, a bit of a law unto herself, was obviously having difficulty in getting used to their new domestic situation. Her relationship with their father's new wife, Shelly, appeared reasonable but she never seemed to show her best side to Chloë.

And Chloë tended to bristle in response.

It didn't help that the girls were opposites – Chloë open, friendly and easy to read, but Melissa more complex, and prone, with her abrupt manner, to giving an impression of being an awkward customer.

Without lifting her eyes from the paper, Melissa extended her arm to return the fragrantly steaming coffee pot to the centre of the table – apparently not realising that she was trying to stand the pot on the edge of a discarded cereal bowl...

'Watch out!' warned Jason.

'What?' demanded Melissa, eyes still fixed to a headline about a merchant bank in London.

'Be careful of the–'

But, too late. Melissa had let go of the coffee pot's handle.

Jason leapt up to try and catch it even as the pot lurched and fell with a clatter on its side. Boiling coffee flooded across the kitchen table.

'Oh *no!*' Melissa leapt up, too, grabbing the pot back onto its base.

Simultaneously, Chloë reached for Patrick, whipping Patrick's royal blue polo shirt up over his head, leaving him bare chested and startled. '*Patrick!* Are you OK? Did it hurt you?'

Slowly, looking bemused, Patrick shook his head. 'It didn't have time to soak through to my skin. You were dead quick. But look at my comic! It's sopping!'

'Don't worry about that.' Jason took the steaming shirt out of Chloë's hands, shaken to feel the temperature of the material where the coffee had now soaked in. 'We need to thank Chloë. The speed she yanked that off you saved you from a nasty scald.'

'Yes, thank you Chloë – oh-oh.' Patrick's expression became fixed.

Jason slipped a friendly arm around his little brother's slight body. '*Oh-oh* what?' He couldn't help grinning. He knew that *Oh-oh*. It came out when Patrick realised he'd forgotten to finish his project for school, or kicked a ball through a window accidentally. Jason had smoothed over a host of *oh-oh* moments for Patrick.

'Oh-*ohhhh*,' repeated Patrick. And he pointed at the chair beside him. 'Coursework.'

'*Oh no!*' wailed Chloë. And then, with a little scream, 'My *coursework!*'

Immediately, a stricken look fell across Melissa's face. 'Oh *no!*' she echoed. 'Chloë, that was completely my fault, I'm so sorry–'

Chloë whirled, furious tears starting in Chloë's eyes and her hands clenched to fists by her sides. 'I'll just *bet* you are! Yes – I bet!'

There was a silence.

'I hope you don't mean you think I deliberately–!' Melissa began hotly.

Swiftly, Jason jumped into the argument. 'Chloë, Melissa would never do anything so underhand as to destroy all your hard work on purpose. You can take my word on that.'

'No, she wouldn't,' Patrick agreed.

'Of *course* I wouldn't!' snapped Melissa, in tones of outrage.

Gradually, the fury died from Chloë's face. 'You're right,' she admitted, at last. In silence, she picked up her drenched and smeared work. The paint had shifted down the pages in rivulets, tawny shades mingling sadly with black. She folded them all carefully, smaller and smaller, before shoving them down into the depths of the kitchen bin.

Woodenly she turned and faced her stepsister. 'I shouldn't have accused you of doing something so sly and horrible.'

White faced, Melissa nodded curtly.

Without another word, Chloë picked up her bag and trailed out of the back door.

Jason looked at Melissa. He knew from his sister's set face that she was angry at herself for making such a clumsy mistake. Chloë's accusation would rankle, but Melissa would know she had left herself open to it by not taking the necessary care with the hot coffee. He put his hand on her arm. 'That wasn't very gracious on her part, but she's worked long and hard on her coursework and it's due in today.'

'I *know!* But I can hardly redo it for her, can I?' flashed Melissa, pulling away from his hand. Spinning on her heel, she marched from the room.

Jason turned ruefully to his little brother. 'Oops! But the most important thing is that you weren't hurt. We'd better find you a fresh shirt, eh?'

Patrick rubbed his chest as if suddenly remembering it was bare. 'Oh yeah.'

Jason steered him through the door, just as Ed came down the stairs. He stopped short at the sight of his younger son, eyebrows shooting up into his thick dark hair. 'And what have you been up to, young man?'

'It wasn't his fault,' said Jason, hastily, and explained what had happened.

Ed sighed. 'We could've done without that. Poor Chloë. But poor Melissa, too. I was wondering what had just sent her stomping along the landing.'

'Do you think Chloë and Melissa aren't friends any more?' asked Patrick sombrely.

Jason wondered himself, but he said, 'They'll be OK, I expect. Chloë's upset because of her work, and Melissa ... well, Melissa isn't very good at being in the wrong.'

Patrick heaved a big sigh. 'No. She's tried it before and doesn't like it.'

Even Ed smiled at Patrick's dry remark. 'I'll go up and see she's OK. I'm looking for Emily, as well, I was hoping she was already down here. No? She can't *still* be in the bathroom, surely? That's not like Emily.'

Watching his father run back up the stairs, Jason sighed. He'd been waiting around to get Ed alone to confess what had happened about the car. But now was obviously not a good time.

All the way to school, Chloë blinked back

tears. She didn't even pause at the brook where she normally loved to listen as grasshoppers in the long grass tuned up for a day's music and the water burbled over the shale bed.

She was fuming. Infuriated that she had to do the piece of work and the attendant sketches again – if she could persuade Mrs Meredith to give her an extension. Those blessed tigers! She'd tussled so long and so hard with them. The effort it had taken to capture the loose-limbed stroll and disdainful expression. Hours and hours. So long that she'd used up all the weeks running up to Mrs Meredith's deadline.

So now, instead of a fairly pleasant half-hour in a one-to-one with Mrs Meredith discussing what she was going to do now and how much more work she had to do, she'd have to begin by explaining what had happened. And Mrs Meredith was known to be funny about granting extensions for coursework.

She was angry with herself too. Why had she left the coursework within all too easy reach of splashes and spills? Right beside the breakfast table, for goodness sake, with people coming and going and dashing about in case they were late! Also, she'd let her quick temper betray her. Now she'd have to make it up with Melissa.

Melissa was so spiky.

Crossing the inner quad between the tall buildings that formed the upper and lower schools, Chloë entered the art department and scooted down the corridor to Mrs Meredith's room.

Mrs Meredith favoured what her mother termed 'a bohemian look', which seemed to mean being out of fashion so long her gypsy skirts were back in again, and also her habit of adding thin silky scarves around what was once her waist.

Chloë wasn't certain that the colourful hand-knit chunky cardigans that dipped at the pockets had ever been 'in', but that didn't stop Mrs Meredith from wearing them. This morning her long, frizzy hair spilled down the back of a cherry red one, tissues spilling from one pocket and a pencil poking out from the other.

At least Mrs Meredith never pulled you up about the state of your uniform. She didn't seem to see rips in trousers or yellow paint on black sweatshirts.

Chloë sat down at Mrs Meredith's big worktable with a certain amount of trepidation. Mrs Meredith was one of those teachers who let long pauses develop within conversations, and you had to wait until she spoke again to find out what kind of pause it had been.

As the silence stretched Chloë watched the long fingers, never quite free of ink or paint, checking through a stack of work.

'So,' Mrs Meredith said with a keen look and a suddenness that made Chloë jump, 'do you plan to continue producing work for me of the standard you've managed so far?'

Surprised by this gambit, Chloë nodded. 'Yes, Mrs Meredith.'

A pause. Mrs Meredith extracted a painting, frowned at it, and slid it back into the stack. 'You realise that you have a gift?'

Chloë waited. Mrs Meredith's matter of fact tone made her wonder whether the teacher was complimenting her or whether she was going to suddenly demand why Chloë did so little with this 'gift'. She sat dumbly, her heart picking up speed and a flush darkening her cheeks.

Mrs Meredith pulled forward another stack of work, shaking her head at what she found. 'Well?'

The morning's emotions suddenly foamed up in Chloë's chest. 'But I haven't got my today's coursework to hand in on time,' she burst out. 'I had terrible trouble with the tigers, I've been trying and trying to get them right, and then I left my folder in a stupid place this morning and somebody's coffee got knocked over, and it's *ruined*. I had to throw it all away!' She stopped to push back her hair and discreetly dash the back of her hand over hot eyes to prevent them from leaking tears down her cheeks.

Mrs Meredith paused in her painting perusal to look over the top of her glasses. She waited until Chloë had choked back her tears. 'It's that loose skin on the tigers underneath, isn't it? Did you watch them move? Or work from books?'

Chloë stared. She felt as if a light had been switched on for her. 'I worked from books! But, of course, I should have watched their movements, shouldn't I?'

Mrs Meredith abandoned the work in her hands and extended her fingers into claws, hunching her shoulders up around her neck, making her arms take a couple of long, laconic 'strides'. 'They slink,' she growled, 'they prrrrrrrrowl.' She stopped being a tiger and returned to being a teacher. 'Get a video out of the library and watch it.'

She was reassuringly not angry, so that Chloë felt about to ask, 'Will I be able to have an extension of a week?'

'It's two weeks to the end of term, you can have that. And don't mix it up with your breakfast! And think about protecting it.'

'Thank you!' Thinking the interview over, Chloë picked up her bag.

Abruptly, Mrs Meredith tossed aside the pile of work and waved Chloë back into her seat, dark eyes intent, voice urgent. 'Chloë, listen to me. Garner every mark you can. Work like mad on your coursework, I have high hopes of an A-star result for you. Then, when you leave us, if you decide to go on with your art – and it would be sinful not to – make sure you get onto the best course that you possibly can. I don't know when I last had a pupil who had what you've got – real talent *plus* the right attitude. You're blessed, because neither can be taught.' She smiled slightly as she added, pragmatically, 'There's the bell, you'd better get off to registration.'

Chloë stammered that yes, yes she would, of course, and at least three more *thank you's*. Then left the room to spend the rest of the day in the buzzing classrooms and echoing corridors in a haze of delight. Mrs Meredith thought she had talent! *Real* talent!

The accident to her coursework might

even turn out to be a blessing. She'd watch videos of tigers and she'd learn from the mistakes of last time, and she'd produce better pieces of work. How her tigers would *slink* and *prrrrrrrrowl*...

She returned home that afternoon still walking on air and clutching the video about tigers.

The big old house seemed quiet. She was getting used enough to living there to identify from household noises the likely occupants.

Emily was probably with her beloved pony, Junk, and she knew Patrick had been due to go from school to a friend's house, no doubt to play some game that involved running screaming up and down the stairs as he and three friends had at The Manse last week.

Singing beneath her breath, she called in to the kitchen to say hello to Barbara, busy clearing up after a baking session and possess herself of two of Barbara's legendary melting moments. Then she hurried up to her room with the video.

Prrrrrrrrowl, slink, she thought to herself, as the giant cats idled beneath the trees in their native India on the screen. She turned the informative commentary down – she'd listen later – all she wanted to do for now was scrutinise, study, to get a better idea of how that extra seam of skin fitted the black stripes of the tiger's splendid amber coat together on his chest.

Despite her absorption with the giant cats that could swap their air of world-weary boredom for kitten-like leaps and then, with slash of the tail, turn silent stalker and fast and fierce predator, Chloë gradually became aware of music through the wall. It dawned on her that Melissa must have come home.

She tried to keep her mind on slinking, prowling tigers but it persisted in wandering back to this morning and the ungracious apology she'd rendered her stepsister.

She turned the video off and sighed before making her way to knock on Melissa's door.

She hadn't been in the room much before. It was decorated in strong colours, a deep duck egg blue with apricot accents. The pairing wouldn't have appealed to Chloë, but she had to admit the combination was striking and she could imagine it being of determined, confident Mel's choosing.

Melissa was lying on her bed with a magazine. Music poured from a chrome stereo that flashed like a jukebox.

She looked at Chloë without speaking.

Chloë edged in, wishing Melissa didn't make her feel so young and gauche. She cleared her throat. 'Got a minute?'

Melissa nodded, still watching, not speaking.

Chloë wondered whether she was doing it in the knowledge that it made Chloë uncomfortable and even feel more of the intruder than she felt in this house anyway.

Briskly, Chloë extended her olive branch. 'I was so upset I'm afraid that I didn't accept your apology properly.'

Melissa shrugged. 'Doesn't matter.'

Her stare remained and Chloë thought that if Melissa ever disappeared like the Cheshire Cat from Alice in Wonderland, it would be the stare that was left rather than the smile.

Chloë's gaze was caught suddenly by a picture hanging on the other side of the room. She moved towards it impulsively. 'What a lovely watercolour! Look at the laughter on the child's face and the mischief in that scamp of a dog she's playing with!'

Melissa changed the position of her head to follow Chloë across the room as she closed in on the charming picture.

'My mother, when she was four,' she offered, unemotionally.

'Really? What a lovely thing for you to

have.' Chloë studied the picture for a minute, looking at the light on the long ago Annabelle's hair and the way the terrier crouched, tail awag. Then, without considering her action, lifted a hand to one corner. The broad gilt frame wasn't *quite* straight...

And, almost in slow motion and with a crash noise seemed to go on forever, the picture crashed to the floor.

Glass flew in all directions. The frame parted at three of its corners.

Chloë was left staring in horrified silence at the hole in the wall where the picture hook had once been fixed, and the mess of wood and glass at her feet.

'Oh, *Melissa,* I'm so sorry! I didn't do it on purpose!' Poor Chloë was horrified. 'I barely touched it and it just...' She made a helpless gesture. She felt so *terrible*.

She might've felt better if Mel had ranted and fumed. But Melissa just went white as she stared at the glass a thousand shards and the frame shaken to pieces.

Ed gazed out of the window of his study and into the spacious front garden. Jason should be home soon; Ed wanted to talk to him.

Whilst he waited for his son to appear he thought of his new wife, the sticky moment over Shelly's job fresh in his mind.

He'd never meant to upset Shelly and had been taken aback by her tart reaction. He'd thought he'd been doing a nice thing, offering her a chance to slow down. Most women would...

Most women would ... would they? He rubbed his chin. Perhaps most women wouldn't. And it didn't really matter what *most* women would like. He should just concern himself with Shelly. At the bottom of him he knew that if Shelly wanted to make some change to her working life she would have gone ahead and done it. That was Shelly.

Annabelle had been different, a happily stay-at-home wife.

Besides bringing the children up Annabelle had been a governor of their school and organised pretty much any fundraiser she'd felt needed organising. She'd also enjoyed cooking, entertaining, and gardening. She'd expressed no wish for a job outside the home.

A career.

He thought with fondness of the mother of his children, Annabelle who had died so young. But Annabelle was in the past and he'd finally moved on from her death and was married to a very different woman now. A woman who had a wide ambitious streak, and could combine her heady working life admirably with the needs of her daughter, Chloë.

The more he thought about his offering her a job at Avenue Windows, the more he saw it had been the wrong thing to do. He hadn't thought deeply enough about suggesting that she 'downshift' – he'd simply seen her long hours and judged them unnecessary.

He, after all, earnt enough for both of them… He groaned, and his conscience twanged. If he was brutally honest with himself, he'd made his suggestion because he wanted to see more of her, not because it was what was best for her, or what he thought she'd want.

He'd wanted her to be at home more and had simply tried to make it happen. That was his way, to make things happen.

Annabelle had always seemed content that he should be the driving force in the relationship. He'd enjoyed it when she'd sought his advice about almost any decision.

But, he thought, gazing out almost unseeing at the smooth green of the lawn fringed with yellow roses, Shelly wasn't Annabelle. She was quite another person, and with clear and reasoned and definite opinions.

Trying to impose his views on her would cause ... friction.

What was that famous saying? If you love somebody, set them free.

Shelly was used to her independence and had worked hard for her career. He should accept it – in fact, he should be proud of her.

His eyes sharpened as Jason finally lounged through the gateway in the fir trees. A backpack hung from one shoulder, his blue school shirt ballooned around him – Ed wished he could break him of the habit of wearing shirts two sizes too big – and his grey and blue school tie dangled from his trouser pocket. It was better not to think where his expensive school blazer had ended up, but the backpack looked suspiciously plump.

Ed wandered into the large, square, tiled hallway to intercept his eldest son. 'Hello, Jason! Got a few minutes for a chat?'

'OK.' Jason looked wary, but he followed his father back into the study.

Ed dropped into one of the big tan leather armchairs in front of the fireplace. No fire burnt now, of course, and the fire basket was full of papery dried flowers in subtle colours. 'So, have you had your interview at that garage?'

Jason nodded. 'Just now.'

'How did that go?'

'I start tomorrow at eight. When the holidays begin I'm going to work full time.' There was an unmistakable note of pride in his voice.

Ed looked at Jason. So nearly a man, but so much a child, so open to misjudgements, so few experiences to call upon. But, oh how reluctant he was to take advice or help! Especially, most especially, from his father.

'Congratulations,' Ed said, mechanically. 'I'm disappointed you don't want to work for Avenue Windows any more, of course.'

'We're only talking the summer, Dad. I just want to have a go at something different. To be somewhere where I'm not the boss's son.'

Unreasonably slighted, Ed protested. 'I wouldn't say I've given you special treatment!'

Jason laughed, his eyes lighting up. 'Neither would I! But the workforce treat me specially, I assure you. They don't give me a deliberately hard time but they make it obvious that there's a *them* and *us,* and I'm *them.* They watch what they say, there are no silly jokes on whatever crew I'm on. They're afraid I'm going to run to you with tales.'

Ed waited for him to go on. Jason, of all his children, was the one who played his cards close to his chest. It wasn't just that he bottled up his feelings – he did – but he kept things from his father, seemingly for the heck of it. Jason was a good boy but, for some reason, he liked his secrets.

He tried not to mind that Jason was growing up, but he couldn't help caring, just a little bit, that Jason hadn't told him about the garage job. Kenny Brannigan had. When challenged, Jason had just shrugged. 'I would've told you once I knew I had the job.'

'So,' Ed tried to make his voice jovial, 'you're convinced you'll like working at the garage better, are you?'

Jason shrugged. A shrug was his irritating response to many a question. 'I'm going to be a nobody there, Dad. No one will stop what they're saying when I arrive, or watch their language, or get a sudden attack of industry. I'll just be Jason the Grease Monkey, and it won't matter that I'm Ed Wright's son.'

Ed felt his heart sink. 'And being Ed Wright's son is bad, is it?'

Jason grinned suddenly, a grin that lit up his sensitive face like a shaft of sunlight as he gave his father a mock punch on the arm.

'No, Dad, it's great. I just want to see how I get on without that insurance.'

At the end of Jason's first day at Pearson's Garage, he was tired but happy. The young lads talked about how they were going to spend their wages. The older and steadier made plans for shows and outings.

'Have a last go round, Jace, then we'll toddle off.' Kenny passed Jason the broom. Jason was getting quite familiar with that particular item, having already swept the repair shop and forecourt once that day. Like everyone else, Jason wore navy blue overalls and had oil ingrained into his hands even if his was from passing tools and parts for the skilled men rather than wielding so much as a wrench himself.

But he was happy. Happy at being around cars, happy at the sound of an engine and the smell of old oil draining out of a sump.

When the sweeping was done, Jason prepared for the walk out of town towards The Old Manse, calling goodbyes and pausing to have one last word with Kenny.

But Kenny's attention quickly drifted away from Jason. 'Hello. Looks like you're wanted.'

Jason turned to see his father bearing down on him purposefully. 'What's he doing here?'

Ed didn't look particularly happy. He exchanged unsmiling but courteous greetings with Kenny then fixed an intent gaze on Jason. 'Does the name Ralf Hangar mean anything to you?' Anger threaded his voice.

Kenny, who'd been in the act of turning away, turned back.

Jason swallowed. He'd hoped to sort things out without his father needing to know. But it was obviously too late for that. 'I was going to see him tomorrow,' he offered.

'Well, Mr Hangar obviously got tired of waiting. He's just rung the house. It seems he's a bit annoyed with you. What have you got to say about it?'

Kenny cleared his throat awkwardly. 'I know Ralf Hangar, he's a good chap. If I can help at all...'

A long moment before Ed shifted his gaze from Jason's hot face. 'Thank you, Kenny, perhaps you can. Mr Hangar informs me that Jason has shaken hands on a deal to buy a 1959 Ford Anglia!'

Kenny's eyebrows shot up. 'Have you, Jace?'

Jason cleared his throat and shoved his hands into his pockets. 'A 105E Deluxe, Imperial Maroon. I was going to buy it from Ralf–'

'Going to?' interrupted Ed. 'You'll have to buy it.'

'You've shaken hands on it!' said Kenny, simultaneously. Jason saw the two men exchange glances as if noting that they evidently felt alike on this.

But his main focus, right now, was on a different aspect of the subject. 'Yes, but then I found out about the insurance, as you said, Kenny. None of the classic car companies will insure me until I'm at least 21.'

Kenny frowned. 'I suggested you speak to the insurance company, but I never suggested you should agree to buy a car before talking to your dad!'

'What on earth do you want with an old banger, anyway?' broke in Ed.

'Oh, Dad, it's not a banger, it's a classic car! It's got that cool reverse-rake rear screen and a "big smile" grille–'

Ed's brows snapped down. 'I know what a Ford Anglia looks like, thank you! What I mean is, why on earth did you buy it? A modern car would be much more sensible! And now you're stuck with this.'

Jason was fast coming to the same conclusion. He'd definitely leaped before he'd looked on this one. Uneasily, he shuffled. 'I was going to see Ralf tomorrow and explain,' he began.

'What? Weasel out of it?' his father exploded.' Oh no, you don't, Jason! No son of mine will welch! Mr Hangar has turned away other buyers on the strength of your agreement, and he's already had to wait longer than arranged. You've agreed to buy the wretched thing, you'll have to darned well buy it! A car you can't drive? Well, perhaps that'll teach you a lesson about doing things behind my back!'

Swallowing hard, Jason looked down at the asphalt forecourt. 'Yes, Dad.' He was beginning to wish now that he had never laid eyes on Ralf Hangar's 105E Deluxe.

'It's not a bad car, if it's the one I'm thinking of,' Kenny observed. 'Nothing serious wrong with it. But Ralf's getting on and he hasn't looked after it as it deserves this last year or two. How about if I put young Jason right on how to tidy it up? Then I can help him sell it again. I can probably make him a few bob on it then he'll have that much more to spend on a more up to date runaround.'

Slowly, Ed turned to look at him. 'That's a very generous offer, Kenny.'

Kenny scratched his chin. ''Course, it'll mean that if he passes his test next week he won't have anything to drive, until the

Anglia's sold.'

'That would be something he'd just have to put up with. *Wouldn't* you, Jason?'

'Unless I can borrow Shelly's little…?' Jason met his father's eyes and got his answer. He would not be borrowing Shelly's little car. 'Yes, Dad.' His visions of driving himself around faded into some unspecified future date.

Shelly Wright pulled into the car park of *Fitt'n Well,* switched off the engine and surveyed the property. *Fitt'n Well* was a client fresh to the agency and the senior partners felt the fitness studio would fit well with her list.

For one thing, the premises were literally down the road from her new home just off the tree-lined main road that was a mass of blossom in springtime.

The yards of plate glass that surrounded the swimming pool were coated with some blue, reflective material that acted like a mirror from the outside and provided the pool users with a peaceful glow. The banks around the car park had been landscaped, great cushions of flowers making *Fitt'n Well* a pretty asset to the mainly residential street.

She followed two women in track suits and

trainers through the entrance doors, impressed immediately by the pale pink and blue décor, the flourishing plants and the relaxed atmosphere. She was shown in to meet Mandy Fitton who looked incredibly young with her hair swinging in a ponytail, sparkling white jazz shoes on her feet.

'Hi, hi, come in!' she beamed. Friendly and energetic, her enthusiasm was obvious. She was also astute enough to have done her homework. 'I've prepared this material for you – our current brochure, a summary of our classes: yoga, Pilates, all kinds of aerobics and dance...'

Shelly turned the pages of the presentation folder. 'That's really helpful.'

Mandy bounced to her feet. 'I'll show you around the place, so you can get a feel for us.'

'Brilliant!' Shelly followed Mandy into the pale pink mirrored studio where an aerobic class was in full swing – it had been a long time since she'd been to such a class. She felt a sudden nostalgia for the exhilaration of bouncing around in a leotard and trainers.

By the time she'd studied the whole set up and talked exhaustively to Mandy and her partner, Kimberley Wells about what the agency could do for them, it was almost seven in the evening. Mandy and Kim still seemed as fresh as the proverbial daisies. Probably they hadn't begun work until the pool opened at noon as the evenings would be their busy time. But Shelly had been on the go since breakfast and she was quite glad that she only had a three-minute drive to get home.

At least she would be in time for dinner. She checked her watch – no she wouldn't! But maybe the others wouldn't have quite finished. She knew Ed wasn't happy when she was late for the family meal but sometimes it just couldn't be helped. The clients had been so excited and enthusiastic about raising the profile of their business. She pulled out of the car park and onto the main road.

Once home, she discovered only Ed left at the table, turning over the pages of the evening paper as he sipped coffee from a white and gold china cup.

'Late!' she cried. 'Sorry, darling.'

He smiled, and accepted her kiss. 'Your meal's in the oven.'

Shelly fished the hot plate out and returned to sit with her husband. 'Good day?'

He sighed and pulled a face. 'Bit of a problem with young Jason.'

She listened as he related the story of the

agreement that Jason had recklessly rushed into and Kenny's generous solution.

'You have to admire Kenny's standards. And he's not scared of work,' he allowed. 'Even if he's never...' He halted as Chloë dashed into the room.

'Hi Mum! Mwah!' She pressed a big kiss on Shelly's cheek. 'I'm going with Emily to see her pony, can I leave you this form to say you've read this letter about school uniform? See you later!'

Shelly laid down her knife and fork, scanned the letter then signed the form before reminding Ed of the sentence he'd broken off. 'Even if he's never what?'

Ed hesitated. 'Doesn't matter.' He looked uncomfortable.

Shelly felt a sudden dart of anger on Kenny's behalf. Kenny might not be ambitious, but he was a good man. 'Even if he's never got very far?' she finished for him. 'Never made much money? Never made his mark?'

'I never said any of that,' Ed said slowly. 'He's obviously a decent bloke and as honest as the day's long. Anyway,' he added, pouring them both coffee. He tapped the paper Shelly had just set aside and smiled bleakly. 'He's made his mark all right. In case you hadn't noticed, your name is Mrs Wright. You've just signed that note "Shelly Brannigan."'

Chapter Four

Chloë threaded her way through the noisy market, pausing to joke with Irenie from the veg stall and Henry from homemade pickles and jams. The green striped stall canopies swelled in the breeze and the aroma from the burger van made her suddenly hungry.

She often took this route after school on a market day.

It wasn't far out of her way and she sometimes had the time to stop and help Philly.

'Can you use some help to pack up?' she called now, as she spotted Philly's colourful figure behind a stall halfway up a row. Chloë enjoyed stowing away Philly's trays of glassy jewellery into the racks Kenny had fitted inside the van or slotting small boxes neatly into larger ones while the stallholders called to each other with end of day cheer.

Philly pushed back her red velvet hat, beaming. 'How about you pop along to the tea stall first, and get us both a cuppa and a doughnut?' She dropped some coins in Chloë's hand.

Many of the stallholders were pausing to refresh themselves before they fetched their vans, and Chloë had to queue for her cardboard tray of steaming cups and greaseproof bag of hot sugary doughnuts. Philly's little white van was in front of the stall, ready, when Chloë returned.

'Just the job!' Philly pulled up a couple of boxes as seats and wrapped her hands around a steaming cup. 'It might be sunny but it's not very warm behind the stall in the shade.' She sighed. 'We don't get our share of sunshine in Britain, that's the trouble, not like some countries.'

'It seemed nice and warm to me, walking home from school. It's only June, after all.' Chloë put her drink down carefully on the edge of the stall. 'You sound as if your itchy feet are bothering you. Still keen to grab your backpack and head into the wide blue yonder?' She spoke lightly, but, inside, her heart was curling as she waited for Philly's reply.

Philly delved into the doughnut bag and came out with a steaming, sugary circlet. 'Ooh, yes! Somewhere warm, with new people, customs, food and sights to see.' Sugar dusted her lips. 'I think if I don't go I'll always regret it. I've got a bit of money saved; I could afford to take time off.'

Chloë made her voice carefully un-concerned. 'How much time, do you think?'

Philly screwed up her face. 'A few months, maybe.'

'A few *months?*' Chloë replaced her doughnut in the bag, appetite disappearing into the hollow that had just grown inside her. 'Is that how long you'll be gone?'

'I haven't made firm plans. Yet.' Philly took another big bite.

'And what about Dad?' Chloë couldn't even sip her drink by now. It would choke her.

'We haven't gone into it.' Philly's eyes were alight. 'But it would be brilliant to start planning, wouldn't it?'

'I suppose so, if you hanker after that kind of thing.' Chloë managed a smile, and turned to lifting skeins of glass beads from the hooks at the side of the stall. The beads blurred, until all she could see was a kaleidoscope of colours.

Philly chatted on brightly about the rivers of India and the temples of Japan, and, 'Oh yes?' answered Chloë. 'Really?' And she was grateful when Ricky from the stall at the end of the row interrupted, and so she didn't have to listen to the wonders of faraway shores any more.

'Here you are, Chloë! This is what you wanted.' He passed her a flat parcel. 'You're doing a grand job behind there – want to come and work for me?'

'Oy,' laughed Philly, 'hands off my helper! I've paid her with a doughnut!'

Chloë smiled at the banter as her hands worked mechanically at untangling hipster belts of leather laces and turquoise beads but, for once, she couldn't wait to set out for home.

Home. It was probably the first time she'd thought of The Old Manse as home. And she had to acknowledge to herself, as she turned into the wide drive later, that she was beginning to feel comfortable there now she was familiar with the household. Who could fail to be comfortable when every comfort was provided? The Old Manse was warm, cheerfully decorated and full of mod cons. She lifted her hand to the big central door knob.

But she let it fall as a splash of blue caught the corner of her eye amongst the pink blossoms of the big cherry tree at the corner of the house, and she recognised the colour of

Emily's school sweatshirt. 'Emily?' She put down her school bag, careful of the parcel she'd stowed in one side, and trotted over to the tree. 'Have you hidden yourself up there for any particular reason?'

Shading her eyes against the sun that flickered through the blossom, she registered the telltale redness around Emily's eyes. 'It looks lovely and cool up there.' She pretended not to have noticed. 'Can I come up?'

Emily shrugged. But, after a moment, she inched along her broad branch to make room.

The trunk was smooth but the many branches made it almost as easy to scale as a ladder. Chloë was soon up beside Emily. 'Wow, it's another world up here! Like being inside a bouquet. Thanks for letting me come up.'

'S'OK.' Emily let out a long sigh.

Chloë made her voice sympathetic but not, she hoped, big-sisterish. Having watched Melissa and Emily at loggerheads, she was aware that big-sisterishness didn't go down well with Emily. 'You look upset. Are you in trouble with your dad?'

Wordlessly, but her face heavy with woe, Emily shook her head.

'You've been awfully quiet lately. Is it

school? Forgotten your homework, or fallen out with a friend?'

Emily sniffed and one big tear slipped slowly down her cheek. 'It's Junk.'

Chloë was alarmed. 'Your pony? Is he ill? Your dad will get the vet–'

But Emily was shaking her head again. Her dark eyes were big and tragic. 'I've…' She had to take another couple of breaths before she could choke it out. 'I've *outgrown* him.'

For a few seconds, Chloë struggled to comprehend the significance of the words. It made sense that children outgrow their ponies, and then…

'Oh,' she mouthed. 'So what happens when you outgrow a pony?'

Dashing the back of her hand angrily across her eyes, Emily snapped, 'What do you think? They get *sold!*'

After dinner, Chloë followed Melissa upstairs. She fetched the parcel that Ricky from the market had passed to her that afternoon, and tapped on Melissa's door. When she went in, Melissa was lying on the bed with her homework.

Melissa raised one eyebrow. 'This is an unexpected honour.'

Chloë willed herself not to colour up. She

99

often was uncertain whether Melissa was being off with her or if it was just her manner. 'I brought you something.'

And she watched as Melissa hesitated, took the parcel, then rolled over to rip the bubble wrap from it.

Chloë began to back towards the door. 'I know you were upset when I broke the painting of your mother. I got it reframed for you,' she explained. 'I hope you like it. It's quite a close match to the original.' By this time she was ready to step out and shut the door behind her.

'Chloë!' Melissa's voice halted her. Then she smiled. 'Thanks. It's cool.'

And Chloë smiled back, glad she'd made the effort to replace what she'd broken.

Ed enjoyed the half-hour before dinner; it was a chance to wind-down. He liked it even better when Shelly was home to join him in the study for a sherry. 'Garden looks nice,' he observed, nodding through the glass of the French doors at the smooth lawns and the drifts of mulberry-coloured tulips between the trees.

'Beautiful.' Shelly, curled in a big leather chair, also looked beautiful with her hair newly brushed and falling onto the shoulders of a pretty cotton top.

He looked up as the study door opened. 'Chloë? Come on in your mother's here.'

Chloë, her long dark plait swinging, edged in. She flickered a brief smile at Shelly but then turned to Ed. 'Actually, I need a word with you.'

He felt his smile broaden. Whatever was on Chloë's mind, he was happy to be the one she'd come to. He so wanted to form a bond with his wife's daughter but he seemed to have been ham fisted about it so far. Shelly had told him not to try so hard. To give Chloë time to get used to things. So he was deliberately casual when he asked, 'Something I can help you with?'

Dropping down onto a leather footstool, Chloë considered him gravely. 'I don't want to tell tales.'

He nodded slowly. His children were very keen on not telling tales – probably Chloë, an only child until pitched into the Wright family, was unsure about exactly how that worked. 'I'm sure you won't be.' He winked. 'And if I think there's any danger that you are, I'll pretend I haven't heard. OK?'

Faintly, Chloë smiled. Then she frowned. Then sighed. 'It's Emily. She's unhappy, but she doesn't want you to know. But I think you *ought* to.'

He sat up, the leather chair creaking. 'I think you're right! Who's making her unhappy? What are they doing?'

'It's not a person. It's Junk.'

'Ah. *Junk.*' Slowly, he sat back.

'She says she's outgrown him.'

He nodded. 'I'm afraid she has already. I've seen this problem coming – she's put on such a spurt lately, you can almost see it as you watch.'

Shelly glanced from him to Chloë. 'Sorry to be dim, but why, exactly, is that making her unhappy?'

'I'm afraid it means he'll have to be sold. It's a hazard with ponies. Emily's so mad about him that she's going to find it heart-rending to see him replaced with something more suitable.'

Shelly sipped her sherry. 'Oh dear! Now I see why she's so unhappy. And he has to be sold, does he?' Her eyes were plainly saying, *It's not as if you're short of money...*

He smiled, sadly. 'I'm afraid he does. Emily's only ten, she could grow out of three ponies before she's finished. We can't keep them all – we'd have a herd! And Junk would become unhealthy with nobody to ride him; he's far too young to be put out to pasture.

No, Emily knows the score; we talked about this day coming. But it won't be easy for her, poor darling. Poor old Em.' He pictured the light that shone in his younger daughter's eyes whenever she so much as mentioned her pony. The image squeezed his heart.

'Thanks for letting me know, Chloë. You did the right thing. I'll be as gentle with her as I possibly can.'

All through dinner, Ed watched Emily.

She was quiet and her white face and reddened eyes told their own story. His other children glanced at each other, but all managed to refrain from demanding explanations.

Inwardly, he groaned. The situation had to be handled delicately; it wasn't something to be rushed into. As her father, he was achingly aware that Emily regarded Junk as her dearest friend. It would hurt her to see him go.

He surveyed his family, thoughtfully. Jason, in taking this job at Kenny's garage, had proved his reluctance to accept Ed's guidance. Jason might often seem content to let others have their way but his mettle showed in the form of stubbornness from time to time. Shelly had made her independence equally clear. Melissa – well, Ed and Melissa butted heads on many occasions;

she was a chip off the old block, that one, absolutely certain of her own judgement at all times.

Young Patrick, of course, was as happy and heedless as only an eight year old boy could be.

But *Emily*. Emily was his little girl, and she needed him to help her face the difficult truth that she simply couldn't keep a pony she was too big for. It was unfair to Junk.

Kenny Brannigan stared at Philly. 'What's brought this on, all of a sudden?'

Philly, a vision in a purple velvet skirt and lacy silver top, grinned. 'Oh come on, Kenny, it's not all of a sudden! It's something I've wanted to do all my life, I've often talked about it.'

'True,' Kenny acknowledged. 'But I thought talk was all it was.'

Philly laughed. 'I'm just beginning to think that if I don't get on with it, the opportunity might pass me by.' She clasped her hands. 'Haven't you always wanted to see different countries and explore their traditions?'

'Not specially,' he admitted, frankly. 'And I don't think it was best to talk to Chloë about it before talking to me, either.'

She wrinkled her nose. When she wrinkled

104

it like that it turned up and put Kenny in mind of a wayward elf. 'I hadn't planned to, but Chloë brought it up.' Philly's eyes were clear and compelling. 'And my feet started itching. I'm ready to start planning my route!' She jumped out of the chair and snuggled down beside Kenny on the sofa. 'How about it?'

Kenny slipped his arm around her, trying not to let his lack of enthusiasm show. 'What, how about me going with you, do you mean?'

She planted a big kiss on his cheek. 'Yes, of course that's what I mean! What else? Wouldn't you just love it, Kenny? Freedom to roam, seeing how other folk live? It would be brilliant for us to go together but I know you can't take that much time off. How about I go first, then you join me for a while?'

He looked into her vivid, hopeful face, and his heart melted. 'I suppose it might be possible,' he allowed. 'If I took a couple of weeks of unpaid leave to add to my summer break in the school holidays, I *could* see if Shelly will let Chloë come along. Not that I'm confident that she will, not for such a long holiday.'

Philly's beaming smile faded a little. She hesitated, before saying, awkwardly, 'I wasn't thinking of taking Chloë, Kenny. You know I think the world of her, but freedom's the name of the game! We might have to be adventurous, rough it a bit – we don't want to be worrying about a young girl. She'll be safe at home with Shelly and Ed; you won't have to be concerned about her.'

Kenny shook his head. 'Not take *Chloë?* I know that she would be safe with Shelly and Ed, of course she would! But there's no way I'm going to leave her for a whole month – she's gone through a difficult enough period, I don't want to go jazzing off to France or somewhere on a glorified holiday.'

Philly flushed. '*France?* France is only next door! No, I was thinking of Thailand or New Zealand. Or India!'

Kenny snorted. 'You can say goodbye to that idea then because I'd never go so far from her for that long!' He paused to gather his thoughts. 'Philly, it would tear me apart. You haven't got children of your own, you just don't appreciate how deeply a parent loves them. I'm not at all sure I want to *rough it,* anyway. Who'd leave a comfortable home to sleep on the floor of a titchy tent?' Then, his conscience bothering him at the vehemence of his reaction, he added, 'I'm sorry to disappoint you.'

But Philly was drawing away from him, eyes fixed on his lips, for once in her life, a flat, unsmiling line. 'Pardon me for being so insensitive, and for wanting to do something more interesting than trailing around yet another autojumble!' She snatched up her thick homemade cardigan from the back of a chair, the one with the big cross stitch running down the sleeves. 'You stay safe in your house, polishing your cars, Kenny. I'll send you a postcard.'

'But, Philly–' he protested, alarmed suddenly at the anger in her eyes.

'Sorry – I've got a big trip to plan!' And Philly swept out of the room, leaving a thick silence behind her.

Kenny stayed where he was. He knew there was no point going after Philly, not when she was in high dudgeon like that. He'd only make everything worse. Crikey, he'd mishandled that! He ought to know how much the prospective trip meant to Philly. She, free spirit that she was, had always boasted she was going to travel one day. But, he supposed, he'd kind of hoped that day would never come.

And now she was disappointed in him because he didn't want to drop everything to chase off across another continent.

He wished the women in his life would just blessed well accept him as he was! When he'd been married to Shelly she'd wanted him to be ambitious, and now here was Philly, expecting him to develop wanderlust!

An hour later, Kenny stirred as he heard the sound of Chloë's key in the front door. 'Hello! All alone?' She glanced around the room and into the adjoining kitchen. 'No Philly? I thought you and her were cooking chicken curry? I've brought the naan bread.'

Kenny shook himself out of his thoughts. 'Philly can't join us tonight, after all. So we'll have to tackle the curry alone.'

His daughter fixed her keen gaze on him. 'Are you OK, Dad?'

'Of course. Let's get the chicken out of the fridge, shall we?' He pasted on what he hoped was a convincing smile. 'I'll wash the chicken, while you begin on the onions.'

He tried to act normally, to ask about Chloë's day and chat as usual, but it was difficult when he felt so bruised inside. And empty.

And he knew that Chloë wasn't fooled. In fact, the more he chattered, the quieter she became. Until, finally, she demanded, 'What's the matter?'

'Why should anything be the matter?' But he knew that his hearty voice wasn't coming off. So he turned the heat down beneath the curry sauce, and pulled Chloë into his arms for a hug. He sighed.

'I'm afraid it looks as if Philly and me have come to a parting of the ways. I wasn't able to do something she wanted me to do and I might have handled my refusal a bit clumsily. She left, and the way it sounded, I don't think she'll be back in a hurry.'

Chloë returned his hug, pulling his shoulder tightly against her cheek. 'Was it to do with the travelling, Dad?'

He sighed. There wasn't much you could keep from Chloë. 'I'm afraid so. It showed up our different values. Philly has no children. It's impossible for her to understand completely how parents automatically put kids first. I can't leave you behind.'

He kissed the top of Chloë's head, his heart aching a little to see a vibrant red clasp from Philly's stall holding back his daughter's hair.

After a long minute, Chloë pulled away. Her voice was firm, but her eyes were too bright and shiny to convince him that she was happy. 'I'll be OK if you want to go with her, Dad. You and Philly care so much about each other!'

He took her hands. 'But that's the thing. Do we? When we want such different things and won't compromise for each other? Because I simply don't want to go traipsing around the globe! It would mean not seeing you for a month, or even longer, the way she was talking. And that's just too long. It's not that I feel a duty to be near you – I simply can't bear *not* to be. And that's a distinction that Philly can't see. And, anyway, I'm not certain I'd want to go even if you were older and had gone away to university – with all her talk of adventures and roughing it, she didn't make it sound that appealing!'

Ed drove grimly, and faster than usual.

He slid the car into small gaps in the traffic to save fractions of seconds. When he reached the car park – frustratingly full, he had to drive round twice before finding a space – it was all he could do to control himself long enough to sift out the correct change and buy a ticket from the big orange machine, cursing the strictly adhered to pay and display system. The instant that the ticket was safely affixed to the inside of the windscreen, he slammed the car door and set off at a run for the big double doors that were signed: *Accident and Emergency.*

At reception, he rapped out, 'My daughter's been brought in – Emily May Wright.' And in minutes he was in a small room containing a trolley. And Emily was lying motionless upon it.

He halted, the room swimming around him as he watched a doctor stoop over his daughter, lifting her eyelids and shining a light into her eyes.

Emily, perfectly still, small and defenceless in her riding breeches, did not respond. Ed recoiled to see a swelling and a livid red mark curving from her temple towards her ear, and a small oxygen mask over her mouth and nose.

The nurse who'd brought Ed in announced quietly, 'Mr Wright, Emily's father, is here, Dr Groom.'

Before the words were out of her mouth, Ed was beside Emily, gazing down at her white face and taking her cold little hand in his. 'Emily, darling?'

'Ah,' said Mr Groom, putting away his little light. 'I'm not quite sure how much you've been told, Mr Wright, but Emily has taken a nasty knock to the head.'

Ed felt something cold squirm inside him. 'She came off her pony, I understand. She was riding with two older girls, and they had

111

the sense to call an ambulance, and then me.'

Dr Groom, a middle-aged man with a slow smile, nodded. 'Mobile phones have their uses, eh? The ambulance got to her quickly, which is good, but, as you can see, Emily is unconscious at the moment. The other girls think she might have been caught a blow by the pony's hoofs, and I'd agree that that is most likely. She was wearing a helmet, which is in her favour.'

'I insist on that,' Ed put in numbly.

'Saved her from worse injury, then. But it looks as if the hoof still caught her just under the rim of the helmet and so hit her quite a blow. I don't think we can necessarily expect to see her rousing just yet awhile.' He hesitated. 'Don't be too alarmed, but we're going to take her straight up and put her on a ventilator.'

Ed swung on him in horror. 'A *ventilator?* But she's breathing!'

The doctor's voice was low and measured. 'It's not because she can't breathe alone – that's only one function of a ventilator. At this stage, it's crucial that we ensure as much oxygen to the brain as practicable. It will help her over the next few days. And we will be monitoring Emily very carefully.'

It seemed no time until Emily was in bed

in a white and cream room, dressed in a cotton gown, the sucking of the ventilator loud in the hush.

She had not stirred.

Ed sat numbly beside her. How could somebody so energetic, so vital as Emily, be so still for so long?

He sat there, Emily's little hand cool and lifeless in his. Then the door behind him opened and Shelly crept into the room.

'Oh Ed! The poor little darling,' she breathed. 'When do they expect her to wake up?'

Ed shrugged, painfully. 'Not yet, apparently. Probably not today.' Saying the words aloud made the situation uncomfortably real.

He felt his wife's hand stroking his hair gently, rhythmically. It wasn't until she passed him a tissue that he felt the tears on his cheeks.

'Jason, Melissa and Chloë have stayed at home to look after Patrick,' she said, softly. 'They told you not to worry, but to be with Em as long as you need to. They all send their love.'

He cleared his throat. 'Good kids.'

They watched Emily in silence, the dark lashes closed onto her white cheeks. 'I should've got her a bigger pony,' Ed said, gruffly. 'The other girls today were on bigger ponies and poor Junk was trying to keep up with them. Emily shouted that she was going to pull up in a minute but she took one last jump. Junk's knees buckled and he pitched her off.'

'You weren't to know.'

Ed wiped his cheek again. 'I knew the pony was too small for her,' he disagreed. 'But, like her, I was putting off facing up to it. I didn't want to cause her pain. But look what's happened to her,' he finished, bitterly.

Shelly always felt odd when she rang the doorbell of 25 Bryant Street, the house that had been her home in the days when she was married to Kenny.

'Hi,' she said, brightly, when Kenny appeared at the door. 'Chloë left her art portfolio here by mistake. She asked me to pick it up.'

'Sure, come in.' Kenny held the door politely and Shelly stepped inside – into the past, it felt like. The décor had changed in the narrow hall, but the sitting room looked exactly as it had six years ago, when she left. Same suite, same wallpaper, same carpet. Through the little rear window she could see into the garden, where a maroon Ford

Anglia was parked alongside a Corsair. The lawn had become a hard-packed and rutted patch with only a fringe of grass. 'Is that Jason's car?'

'That's right.' Kenny grinned. 'At the weekend I'm going to show him the meaning of elbow grease and how to attend to those rust spots on her brightwork.'

Shelly waited, while Kenny ran upstairs. He was soon down again with the precious portfolio, a flat, zipped black folder.

'Thanks.' Shelly took the portfolio, remembering Kenny buying it for Chloë when he'd made a little money on a car. How proud he'd been to be able to give it to her. How excited she was to have a *proper* portfolio from the art supplies shop. Kenny spent his money carefully and on those he loved.

Impulsively, she said, 'I was sorry to hear about Philly.'

A shadow glided over Kenny's face. 'These things happen.'

'The course of true love never runs smooth.'

'And sometimes it just stops running altogether. How's work, then?'

She accepted the change of subject instantly, aware that talk of love might irritate old wounds. 'Very well, thanks. I'm working more for the main branch of the agency in London, these days. Tiring, but a great challenge.'

He nodded, slowly. 'I might have known you'd still be on the up and up. You didn't consider cutting your work commitment when you married again?'

'Why should I? I'm committed to my job, and I enjoy it.' Suddenly, she felt irritated. 'Look, I don't only work because of economic necessity, you know, I work because I choose to! You do a job you like and Ed does a job he likes – and I'm going to do a job *I* like!'

Testily, Kenny hunched his shoulders. 'Well, it's nothing to do with me any more, is it? And even when it was–' He stopped. Then his face softened. He even smiled. 'Listen to us, getting stroppy about this old chestnut, after all this time!'

Shelly suddenly saw how silly this was. 'Echoes of the past! You'd think we'd learnt to accept each other's different points of view on this one, without squabbling all over again. Thanks for the portfolio. Chloë was panicking until she remembered where she'd left it.'

Outside, climbing into her nice new car, she reflected that Kenny never changed. He

116

honestly could see no reason for her to work as diligently and with such ambition as she did. She smiled as she remembered the day when much anticipated exam results had arrived for her – fantastic results, in fact, distinctions all the way. She'd been so excited that she'd literally danced with glee around the room exclaiming that these results would get her onto part two of her course without question.

And Kenny had exclaimed in tones of horror, 'What? Do you mean *more* studying?'

She'd halted mid-jig, deflating rapidly. 'Of course! Why not?'

His reply had been stiff. 'It's natural for a man to want *some* attention from his wife!'

'And it's natural for a woman to want some support from her husband!'

Oh well. She turned the key in the ignition and listened to the engine fire up. She and Kenny were, and had always been, so different when it came to ambition. But, luckily, Kenny and *Ed* were different, too. Because Kenny would never in a million years understand her need to be challenged every day by her career.

But Ed, now he'd considered her point of view, did.

Jason loped up The Avenue. He'd be glad when he'd passed his test and had his own car – one he could drive, that is, not the 105E Deluxe, Imperial Maroon Ford Anglia currently parked in Kenny's back garden. He ran across the lawn and in through the big black door. 'Dad?'

Into the sitting room, then the study. Spotting Ed in the garden he burst out through the French doors and hurdled down the terraces to where his father was frowning blackly but blindly at a climbing rose.

'Dad? Have you been to the hospital today? How's Em?'

Ed turned, and managed a faint grin. 'She's about the same, Jason. Stable, but it's a long way before she'll be out of the woods.' Again, the frown took up station on his forehead.

Jason pushed back his hair. 'Do you think you'll be selling Junk?'

Ed hesitated. 'To be honest with you Jason, although I know it wasn't the animal's fault, I'm so worried about Emily that I'd *give* Junk away, never mind sell him! But how can I, when she's lying unconscious in hospital? She'd be heartbroken when she came round.' The frown lines carved themselves still more deeply.

Jason knew his father always looked fiercest when he was desperately worried, and placed a comforting hand on his shoulder. 'But even if she hadn't had the accident he would've had to go soon, wouldn't he?'

Shortly, Ed nodded. 'But you know how that would be for poor Em at the best of times, let alone when she wakes up in goodness knows what condition. But, even when she's well enough, she won't be able to ride him any more – it's obviously not safe. He'll just be eating his head off in the paddock and not getting any exercise.' He snapped a dead head from the rose.

Tentatively, Jason said, 'What if there was some way of keeping him, getting him exercised, but you not being out of pocket?'

Ed looked up, eyes narrowing. 'It sounds a bit too good to be true, although being out of pocket is the least of my worries. What have you in mind?'

'There's this boy at school – you know Liam? I went home with him after school today and some of his family were there. His aunt was telling me that her daughter, Lori, rides at a local stables and is a real pony nut. She's seven, and they want to get her a pony – but they don't have anywhere to put it. I told her about Junk, and she said if the pony was up for sale they'd be interested in seeing him, *especially if* you'd think about letting him stay where he is and them paying you for use of the paddock! That way, Em could see Junk every day, but still have a bigger pony, when she can ride again!'

He waited, watching Ed's face. 'That could work very well,' Ed said, slowly. 'Jason, you might've hit on something marvellous!' Even the frown was beginning to be replaced by a tentative smile. 'It could work, it could really work! And there's nothing Em would like better but to have a little protégé to boss about and show her how to clean tack and all that horsey stuff!' He clapped Jason on the back. 'Good lad! That's the beginnings of a weight off my mind!'

'Ed? Ed!' Shelly stepped out of the French doors, a big black zipped folder in one hand, the phone in the other, anxiety on her face. 'Ed, didn't you hear the phone? It's the hospital, for you!'

As one, Jason and Ed swung around and made their way swiftly up the terraces, past stone urns filled with spiky plants, past black wrought iron benches and tables topped with geometric mosaics.

The instant he was close enough, Ed grabbed the phone. 'Ed Wright, here.'

He listened for several moments, before snapping, 'I'm on my way!'

He turned and blundered blindly through the study.

Shelly was right beside him. 'What, Ed? What's happened?'

Jason was only a half-step behind. 'Dad? Is it Em?'

'I've got to go to the hospital!' He fumbled through his pockets for the car keys. 'They need to talk to me as a matter of urgency.'

'I'll drive you!' cried Shelly, sprinting ahead to open the front door. Her face was white and her eyes worried. 'Stay with Patrick, please, Jason.'

Ed could hardly hear his eldest son's assent for the thundering of panic in his ears.

In seconds they were in the little red car, Shelly driving, Ed beside her.

For the first time in many years, Ed found his eyes prickling with hot tears and his throat as tight as if it had turned to elastic that would snap at any moment. And he clenched his fists and willed every traffic light to be green between The Avenue and the general hospital.

In Emily's room, the hospital sounds were muffled. A doctor – Ed was so fearful that he found it impossible even to remember his name – was waiting for them. Emily still lay in bed, but an empty trolley was close beside it.

'She's in a bit of difficulty,' the doctor said, without preamble, as they rushed into the room. 'Our monitors tell us that there's intracranial pressure, pressure on the brain. You'll appreciate that this is a dangerous scenario. The brain is soft and the skull is hard. Allowing the brain to be squeezed against the skull will mean constriction of or damage to small vessels, restricting vital oxygen to the brain – just what we must avoid. We've done a scan and there's a small blood clot *here,*' he placed a diagram beneath Ed's nose and indicated a place with the tip of his pen, 'beside the temporal bone. She needs an operation to remove the clot and ease that pressure, immediately. I need your consent, Mr Wright, to proceed.'

Ed nodded rapidly. 'Make her better! Please!'

The doctor smiled reassuringly as other people entered the room, lifting Emily's small form from the bed to the trolley. 'That's our aim, Mr Wright.'

The medical team gathered protectively around Emily. In seconds they had glided her out through the door and into the corridor. And out of sight.

Ed felt numb all over. Except his heart. That was feeling pain all right.

Chapter Five

Ed sat beside Emily's bed. Around him, machines beeped and hummed and nurses and doctors murmured, their footsteps as hushed as the scratching of their pens in the solemn atmosphere of the Intensive Care unit.

Motionless, he clasped his daughter's hand. The hand was small in his and the nails needed scrubbing. A ten year old who messed about in the stables every day didn't worry too much about her manicure – which was something that normally irritated him. He could hear himself: *Emily, it's not hygienic to carry half the stables around under your nails. Use the nailbrush, that's a good girl.*

Proper use of the nailbrush had ceased to matter, now, with doctors counselling him about *intra cranial pressure* and *anticonvulsants*.

'Any change?'

Too absorbed in his thoughts to have noticed her approach, Ed started at the sound of his wife's voice. Neat but sombre in jeans and a grey T-shirt and her hair back into a glossy ponytail, Shelly patted Emily's leg gently through the white hospital covers. 'Hello, Emily!'

Ed stirred, almost surprised to learn that he could still move after most of the afternoon spent rooted to his seat. 'The doctors are happy that the pressure on her brain has decreased since they put that device in to drain away the excess fluid. They think she's out of immediate danger. I've talked to her until I'm hoarse in case she can hear me. She's opened her eyes several times.'

Shelly sank down beside him with a sigh. 'It seems as if she must be conscious when she does that.'

Morosely, he shrugged. 'But the doctors say not. They won't consider her awake until she can obey commands. Stick out her tongue when asked to, that kind of thing.'

Shelly's hand crept into his. 'It doesn't happen the way it does on the television, does it?'

He snorted. 'Nothing could be further from the truth, apparently. In the movies her eyelids would flutter and she'd look around and say, "Where am I? I'm hungry!"' He shifted uncomfortably in the chair. 'The worst thing about this kind of injury is that recovery is slow and unpredictable. It makes me feel so helpless.' He groaned. 'I made a complete fool of myself this afternoon. A consultant came to talk to me about Emily's condition but he didn't really *know* anything – he said so himself. *There are some positive signs and we must wait and see*, was the best he could offer.' He shook his head. 'For a moment I couldn't bear to wait any longer to have Emily back! I demanded the poor man find an injection or something to wake her up! I said I could pay for any treatment he cared to name, but he must *do* something!'

Shelly's hand squeezed his.

Ed rubbed the bridge of his nose. He seemed to have a permanent headache at the moment. 'He was very nice about it. He said that everything that could be done was being done and he understood exactly how hard the waiting was on the family.'

Shelly lifted her hand and stroked his temples with her cool fingers. 'Money's jolly useful stuff,' she said, gently. 'But there are some things it simply can't buy. Darling, you're under a lot of strain. I want you to come home with me for dinner. Those leaflets the nurse gave us say that the family members of the patient must look after themselves properly and I agree. Emily will need you to be fighting fit when she comes round. And the other children need to see something of you. They're all frightened for Emily, too.'

For a moment, Ed's eyes burned at the love and concern in his wife's blue eyes. 'I'm glad I've got you to lean on,' he said, gruffly. 'And to know that you're looking after everything at home – but you're right about the other children. Young Patrick, especially. He doesn't deserve to be pushed out in the cold.'

Shelly smiled. 'He's sticking to Jason like glue, whenever they're not at school. Jason's playing cards and computer games with him for hours to keep him occupied. Chloë helps, too. She's had them both learning to draw tigers.'

'And I suppose Melissa's doing her lone wolf thing, as usual?'

'Her contribution has been more in the domestic arena, clearing up after meals and that sort of thing – but that's just her way. She's just as anxious about Emily – and you – as Patrick and Jason are, believe me.'

He stretched. 'You're right. I'll come home for the evening. The hospital will phone me if there's any change.' He bent over Emily's little figure, tucked up in the bed. 'I'll be back to see you before bedtime, Emily. Try and get better, darling.' He kissed his daughter's cheek.

Then let his wife lead him out of the cloying hospital atmosphere and into the fresh air.

Chloë trotted up the drive. She'd been helping Mrs Meredith paint enormous yellow and brown caterpillars on big broad leaves for a play the year 7s were putting on. Mrs Meredith always took a big part in set design for school productions and she wasn't shy about roping in talented students to help.

And when Mrs Meredith was involved in a project she tended to give it her complete attention. Timekeeping was only a vague notion to her and Chloë, catching sight of the big chrome clock in the school auditorium, had been forced to wash her brushes hastily and race home for dinner.

'Sorry I'm late,' she panted, as she burst into the dining room where the rest of the family already sat at their places.

Ed, at the head of the table, looked strained and tired. 'You're just in time.'

'Your favourite, darling, cottage pie.'

Shelly passed the carrots and peas and Melissa a steaming boat of gravy as Chloë took her seat.

'Any Emily news?' It was a habit that'd all adopted over the last few days; on coming home all that each of them wanted was to discover if information had come into the house in their absence. And Chloë certainly felt she could scarcely blither on about other, less important things, without asking after her little stepsister.

'Poor Em,' she sighed, as Ed explained that they were still waiting for real progress.

Only when she felt it would be acceptable to change the subject did she turn to Jason, sitting quietly in the place opposite hers. 'Well? How did it go? Did you pass?'

A broad, bashful smile swept over his face. 'I did, actually.'

Chloë clattered her knife and fork to her plate. 'Oh congratulations, Jason, first time! Clever *you!* When you get the Anglia sold you'll be able to…' She stopped, uncertainly, becoming horribly aware of silence. Around the table forks had paused in midair, faces bearing various expressions of dismay.

And then they burst out talking at once. 'Your driving test! You passed!'

'Congratulations, Jason!'

'Cool!'

Jason merely grinned, shaking back his hair.

And then an awkward pause.

Ed, pale and more strained than ever, stared at his first born. 'I forgot about your driving test,' he admitted, hoarsely. 'Son, I'm sorry. That's unforgivable.' Shelly laid a comforting hand over his.

Jason shrugged, colouring hotly. 'It's all right, Dad. I wasn't even sure whether to take it, with Em and everything. But it was all booked and paid for so I thought I might as well... You don't mind, do you?' Chloë could almost feel waves of self-conscious embarrassment emanating from him.

If anything, Ed looked unhappier. 'Of course not! I'm just sorry I forgot—'

'It doesn't matter.' Jason's voice was just a shade too hearty. 'I think it made it easier, actually, there being no fuss. I didn't feel nervous.' He glanced at his watch and changed the subject. 'Get a move on, Patrick, and I'll walk you up to your cubs' meeting.'

Patrick beamed, his freckles standing out like the brown paint spatters all over Chloë hands. 'When you've done up that old car you bought and sold it for another one, you'll be able to drive me!'

'You bet,' agreed Jason good-naturedly. 'Let's go find your uniform. I'll call in at Liam's, Dad, while Patrick's at cubs, then walk him home.' And he followed his little brother out of the room as if glad to escape.

Crushed by Ed's pained expression, Chloë finished her meal in silence, as if, somehow, what had just happened was her fault. She helped Melissa clear the dishes while Ed and her mother remained at the table in low voiced conversation. Once alone in the kitchen with Melissa, she groaned. 'That was awful, the way that worked out. I wish I'd thought to remind your dad. I just assumed...'

'That someone would remember?' Grimly, Melissa finished the sentence. 'I can't believe every single one of us forgot! Normally we'd have a celebration dinner for him or go to the pizza parlour or something. It's just, with Em...' She swallowed.

Chloë glazed at Melissa. Like the rest of the family she looked anxious and ashen. There was a redness around her eyes. Chloë was hollow with worry about little Emily herself, so she could only imagine how much worse it must be for those who were her flesh and blood. She wished she could take their minds off it.

It was a pity that they hadn't arranged a celebration for Jason – it would've given them all something happier to think about for a couple of hours. She cast about for *something* they could do. 'How about if we make him a cake?'

Melissa looked doubtful. 'We'd have to wait for it to cool to ice it, wouldn't we? And do you even know how to make cakes? Because I don't. We'd better ask Barbara to do it, tomorrow.'

But Chloë wasn't easily put off. 'But he passed his test today and it'll mean more if we do it!' She took a big plastic box out of a cupboard. 'There's half a sponge in the cake tin.'

'You can't give someone half a cake!' Melissa almost smiled.

Chloë grinned. 'Of course we can! Let's see what icing sugar and stuff, Barbara has.' She inspected another cupboard. 'Ooh, look, there's food colouring and everything.'

'But it's *half* a cake!' Melissa objected.

'No, it's not.' Chloë picked up the cake and sat it on its cut side so that it rose up in a semi circle. 'It's a car. Or it will be, when we've iced it and stuck on biscuits for wheels.'

An hour of sugary surgery later the car was finished, the bodywork pale blue icing and the windows and bumpers white. The wheels were dark chocolate digestive biscuits. The bonnet and boot bore a 'J' in darker blue.

Melissa inspected it. 'It actually does look a *bit* like a car. Like your dad's.'

Chloë felt pleased. 'Good, because that's exactly what it's meant to be. A Volkswagen Beetle. Lucky for us that a Beetle happens to be about the shape of half a cake.'

'Your fingers have turned blue at the ends.'

'And you've got icing sugar all through your hair. Shall we show the cake to Ed and Mum? Then we can give it to Jason when he comes back in with Patrick.'

Jason walked Patrick home through the dusk, letting his little brother's chatter wash over him. Every so often he would feel a little skip of delight at the thought that he'd passed his driving test. And then an answering tug of sorrow for Em, as if it were indecent to feel happy about anything when she was ill. But he knew Emily wouldn't mind. She'd be pleased he'd passed his driving test apart from anything else it was one more person to give her a lift when she needed one. If she would just get better. And when he got a car. He thought of the Ford Anglia sitting in Kenny's garden, waiting for him and Kenny to begin work on its sprucing up. When it was finished and sold, then Jason could get a car he could drive. It would only be a couple of months, hopefully.

He bitterly regretted his ill-advised foray into the classic car market because there was a little white hatchback on the forecourt of the garage that he would've been able to afford from his savings if he hadn't been inspired to buy a car that had begun life long before he had, and so was impossible for him to insure. The hatchback would've been an excellent buy; it was low mileage and everything.

He couldn't help a small sigh.

'Dad's home,' Patrick observed as they turned into the drive, skipping on the balls of his feet as if he still had energy to burn. 'I thought he would still be at the hospital saying goodnight to Emmy.'

'Yeah, he's not normally back so early.' Jason felt a twinge of anxiety. He quickened his pace.

Indoors, the big hall and most of the rest of the house was in darkness. 'Where are they all?' demanded Patrick.

Jason followed the light spilling from just one door, the study, and was surprised to see the rest of the family gathered there.

'What's the matter?' He looked around, at Ed and Shelly in the armchairs and Melissa and Chloë standing shoulder to shoulder like soldiers in a rank.

Ed smiled. 'The girls have something for you.'

'For Jason Wright, to mark this momentous occasion!' boomed Melissa.

'Tan-*tarrah!*' played Chloë on a make-believe trumpet. And Chloë and Melissa stepped aside with a theatrical flourish to display their cake displayed proudly on a silver salver on the coffee table behind them.

Patrick took a step back. 'Crikey. What on earth is it?'

'It's a car cake!' said Jason, eyeing the blue hump. 'Isn't it?'

'Well, obviously it's a car cake! It's a *Congratulations on Passing Your Test* cake,' declared Melissa with a grin. Some of the wretchedness had left her face.

Patrick promptly stepped forward again. 'Ooh, cake! Can I have a piece?'

'Of course you can.' Chloë looked flushed with pleasure. 'But not a very big slice because it's not a very big cake.'

'It's brilliant, thanks a lot. Both of you.' Jason was touched that the girls had organised this little celebration for him. 'I didn't think I'd be getting a car of my own tonight.'

Melissa produced the plates and Ed and Shelly brought in drinks so that Jason's success was toasted in lemonade or cider, and Jason took a picture of the cake on his little digital camera before his sister divided it up into rather messy portions.

'I'll be able to show the photo to Em, when she's better. I'm sure she won't mind that we didn't save her a piece.'

Ed cleared his throat. He looked slightly more relaxed than he had at dinner. 'Talking about Emily – I've been waiting until we were all together to give you some news. When I went to say goodnight...' He paused to clear his throat once more. 'When I went to say goodnight, Emily squeezed my hand! A doctor came to examine her and we asked her to squeeze it again. And she did!' He gazed around, triumphantly. 'And the doctor said, *We can definitely put that down as a positive response.* So now we've all got something a little more hopeful to think about when we go to sleep tonight.'

Jason really wanted to exclaim, 'That's brilliant!' or, 'The doctor wouldn't say it if he didn't mean it!' But, inexplicably in a person who was so very nearly an adult, his throat tightened around a rod of tears and prevented him from uttering a word. From the silence in the room, it seemed as if he wasn't the only one.

The exception, not surprisingly, was Patrick. 'Perhaps you should have saved her that piece of cake, Jace!' he said, and promptly popped his last bite into his mouth.

As she had done so many times, after school Chloë wandered between the lanes of market stalls, their brightly-striped awnings rustling in the breeze. A couple of the stall-holders called out to her from behind their counters and she waved and smiled in return.

But as she approached Philly's stall her step slowed. She couldn't remember ever being reluctant to see smiling, energetic Philly before, nor expected anything but a friendly reception. But Chloë had no intention of avoiding Philly or the busy marketplace. Philly had been part of hers and Kenny's lives for over a year. This meeting was better confronted and any little awkwardness chased away by the warm friendship there had always been between them.

After all, Philly had had plenty of time to cool down after her disagreement with Kenny.

Chloë was pretty hopeful that Philly and

her dad would get back together again. Philly was such a bubbly, happy person. Chloë had insisted that Philly wasn't the kind of person to hold a grudge. But she'd been surprised when Kenny, quiet and withdrawn, hadn't been so optimistic. 'She's got her quirks, and stubbornness is top of the list.'

Maybe if Chloë could re-establish friendly relations, a thawing of the ice between her dad and Philly would naturally follow?

Philly's stall had a green-striped awning that clashed gaily with her red-streaked hair as she tidied the contents of jewellery trays before sliding their covers in place.

Chloë had been used to walking directly around behind the stall, but today she remained at the front, like a customer. 'Hello, Philly!' She tucked her hands into her jacket pockets.

Philly looked up sharply. 'Oh, hello, Chloë.' Today there was no, 'How are you?', or, 'Let's have a doughnut!' She didn't smile and her hands didn't cease in their methodical work of slipping rings in boxes and untangling skeins of beads.

'Still here, then?' Chloë ventured.

And the instant the words fell from her lips realised that it was quite the wrong thing to say.

Philly flushed. 'For now,' she agreed, shortly. 'But I'm making my travel plans!'

Chloë flushed in return. This was awful! She hated not only such an atmosphere between Philly and herself but, even more, being the cause of *froideur* between Kenny and Philly. 'I was really sorry to hear that you and Dad had a falling out,' she said, carefully.

Silence. Philly's fingers attacked a snarl of brown laces and amber-coloured beads, her eyes fixed on her task.

'It seems such a pity after you've been so close.'

The tangle remained knotted even though Philly yanked and shook at it.

Chloë took a deep breath. 'And it feels like it was because of me.'

Casting the beads and laces aside and taking down a rack of belts, Philly frowned, not meeting Chloë's eyes. 'Hmm. Well. It *is* a pity you had to get your two penn'orth in with Kenny, instead of leaving it to me.'

Chloë's jaw dropped and her heart began to hammer. 'But I didn't–!' she began.

Philly didn't seem in the mood to listen to corrections. 'It certainly set his face against coming travelling. Nothing I could say would get him along!'

'But *I* didn't–!'

138

Holding up both her hands, Philly smiled. It was the first time since Chloë had appeared but it was a sad and un-Philly-like smile. 'Look, Chloë, let's not have a public hair-pulling about it. You're a kid, and you were scared at the idea of your dad going off globetrotting without you. It's understandable. I just hope that as you grow up, you learn that it's better not to interfere in relationships between men and women. Even when you think it's for the best.'

Poor Chloë was miserably lost for words.

'To be brutally honest,' interrupted a cool, composed, and ever so slightly scornful voice at Chloë's shoulder, 'that advice applies rather more to relationships between *father and daughter*. Don't you think that it's a little … *self-orientated*, let alone downright irresponsible, to try and talk a father into leaving his teenaged daughter while he wanders the globe?'

Chloë spun on the spot, unable to speak for shock. *Melissa!* In her spotless blazer and summer uniform, Melissa had appeared beside her.

Philly looked equally jolted. She let a box drop to the stall with a thud. 'I don't think it was quite like that,' she protested.

Melissa's unemotional gaze remained fixed

on Philly. 'It was *exactly* like that,' she con-
tradicted. 'All you cared about was getting
Mr Brannigan on your romantic odyssey.
Strikes me that you didn't much care who or
what you were taking him away from or
whether he wished to be taken. And now it's
caused trouble between you, you're looking
for somebody to blame. And because Chloë
is nice enough to put herself last most of the
time, you thought it might as well be her.'

Ashen, Philly gaped at Melissa. Melissa
stared back. When Philly found no more to
say, Melissa nodded as if satisfied, and
turned to Chloë, completely dumbfounded,
beside her. 'Could you show me where your
father's garage is, please? Jason's working
there this afternoon and I've forgotten to
ask him what time Patrick needs picking up
from after-school cricket.'

Chloë tried to gather her wits. 'Yes. OK.'
She threw one last glance at Philly, who still
looked as if she'd met a Gorgon and been
turned to stone and led the way, wondering
whether she was dreaming.

Or had her prickly stepsister just stuck up
for her?

Jason liked working at the garage for a couple
of hours after school once or twice a week.

140

His dad had made a few doubtful noises about school work, but Jason had pointed out that his AS Levels were behind him and the holidays were nearly here. The garage apprentice would be able to return to the garage in September and Jason would have to concentrate all his efforts on his final year at school.

Throwing his school bag under the table in the staff room, he wriggled into jeans and overalls.

As he emerged into the cool, oily depths of the garage where men lay working beneath cars or stooped over exposed engines, Kenny called out his instructions. 'Two cars want washing, Jace, the white hatchback, first, please. And give it a good go, it's a cracking little car and as good as sold. The customer's coming back before closing for a final look but I think he'll take it.'

'OK, Kenny.' But Jason couldn't help feeling his heart sink. Silly, because he'd known that the white hatchback had been bound to sell before he could realise his investment in the Ford Anglia and buy it himself. Sighing, he unravelled the green hose and filled the big rubber bucket with hot water and the wax wash that would make the car shine. It was his own fault, he knew that. He'd certainly never again shake hands on a deal without investigating the whole picture and even taking the advice of people such as Kenny and his father, who, it had been proved, had a bit more experience of cars than he did. It hadn't taken a minute to tie himself to something he'd since had endless hours to regret.

Still, he thought, as he trickled the hose over the neat little car, Kenny had said they'd begin sprucing up the Anglia on Sunday. He was looking forward to learning how to treat rust spots and tune the old engine.

He dipped a soft-bristled long-handled brush in the bucket of water and began to wash the roof, thick suds sluicing over onto windows as he worked.

When the car was finished he gave it one last longing look and went to fetch fresh water to wash the other car, a silver family estate. He was just running the hose over it gently – he'd long ago discovered that having the hose on more than a dribble meant that all the vehicles around got splashed and made the washer a lot of extra work when a familiar car turned onto the forecourt.

Jason gazed in surprise as his father levered himself from the expensive leather driving seat.

Water continued to run, unheeded, from

the hose in his hand, as he wondered what this meant. Dimly, he was aware of Kenny greeting Ed, turning the tap off at the wall and beckoning. 'Jace!'

With an effort, Jason made his legs carry him over to his father. 'What's the matter? Why are you here? Is it Em?' He fought to keep his voice steady against the cold, sick dread rising in his chest.

But Ed was smiling. 'Emily is still showing signs of improvement. She's becoming more responsive to voices, her eyes opening and her hands moving. The doctor wants you children to talk to her, see if it helps. Perhaps this evening.'

'That's mega!' Jason felt a flood of relief. 'Right. Absolutely, of course we'll go this evening.'

Ed tucked his hands into his pockets and braced his back against the side of his car. 'I've come to talk to you about something else. That Ford Anglia.'

'Kenny says we can begin it this weekend,' Jason said, quickly. He hadn't yet forgotten how displeased and disappointed his father had been over that episode.

'So I understand. Generous of him.'

Jason nodded uncomfortably, not understanding why his father should come to the garage to go over this old ground.

Ed glanced at his watch. 'Look, Jason, this is probably not the right place to do this but our world is upside down at the moment, with Emily being in hospital. You know that I felt lousy yesterday about forgetting your test?'

Jason shifted foot-to-foot. 'But with Emily–'

'Still, I felt awful. And, truth to tell, I think I came down too hard on you about that old car you bought. You're a good lad, and it was a silly mistake rather than a wilful act of bad behaviour. So I'd like to help you buy this car you like, and you can pay me back when the Anglia is sold.'

Speechless, Jason gazed at his father.

'I've no idea how long Emily is going to be in hospital, of course and so in exchange for this favour I'd like you to run Patrick, Melissa and Chloë around when they'd normally ask me for a lift, so that it doesn't all fall on Shelly. How does that sound?'

Swallowing, Jason croaked, 'But you *never* change your mind!'

'We all have to, some time.' Ed clapped Jason gently on the shoulder. 'What do you say? Nice car, isn't it? Kenny let me test drive it this afternoon.'

'It's a cracking little car,' Jason agreed faintly. 'I can't believe you're doing this, Dad! Thanks so much!'

'You're a good lad, and having you mobile will be a help to the entire family over the next few weeks. I've arranged the insurance, all I have to do is make a call now to confirm it and you can drive the car home tonight.' Expectantly, he stuck out his hand.

Jason just looked at it.

Kenny, grinning, called across the forecourt. 'I should shake it, quick, Jace, before he changes his mind!'

'Wow! Yes!' Jason promptly did so. It felt very odd. He couldn't remember ever shaking his father's hand before. After a hesitation, threw his arms around his father, as well. 'Dad, you're a star!'

Ed returned the hug fiercely. 'That must be where you get it from, then. Just do me a favour and drive carefully! OK? I have enough grey hairs.' Ed made the necessary phone call to the insurance company from his mobile and in two minutes was back in his car and away.

In the silence that hung over the forecourt after the big car purred off, Jason turned round slowly to stare at the white hatchback.

Then Kenny was beside him, jingling a set

of car keys. 'You'll need these. Bet you're glad you washed it now, aren't you? Get that other car finished up, then you can knock off and take your car out for a run.'

'My car,' said Jason stupidly.

'Certainly is, boy. And it's a good 'un.'

'*My* car!' Suddenly galvanised into action, with a huge grin Jason turned to the silver estate, washing furiously so that he could get into the fantastic little car and drive around to Liam's or one of his other friends' houses to show off.

And in half an hour he was driving off the forecourt, exulting in the sublime pleasure of driving his first car. It was such a joy that he even forgot to feel cautious about being on the road without an instructor beside him.

But there was part of him that was sober enough to be aware that possession of this little beauty owed a great deal, one way or another, to the injury that had befallen his younger sister. And to wish that good fortune had come to him some other way.

Kenny walked around the Imperial Maroon Ford Anglia sitting beside his Corsair on what once had been his back lawn, thinking about this classic car of young Jason's and planning what to do with it at the weekend.

Faintly, he thought he might have heard his doorbell ring. Chloë and Jason both had plans to go to the hospital; it was probably someone who wanted his help with a vehicle. But it had been a long day and he was enjoying a bit of peace after his solitary dinner.

He was glad that Ed Wright had relented and helped young Jason with the hatchback, even though Kenny was generally one for letting youngsters learn by their mistakes. Jason's face had been a treat when he'd realised that he would be driving home tonight.

Stooping, he ran his eyes over the sills of the Anglia. It was an area where they'd have to do some work. Automatically, he reached for a backboard and lay down on it beside the car so that he could get close enough for a proper inspection, to run his hands over the metal and pick at any suspect spots with his stubby, ingrained fingers. In a moment he was absorbed, moving methodically around the car and noting where rust patches were beginning.

'I thought you might be lurking out here, somewhere.'

Kenny jumped at the sound of the familiar voice, scooting out from beneath the car and rolling quickly to his feet.

And there stood Philly, the plainness of black jeans thrown into relief by a rainbow of a scarf serving as a belt and an alphabet T-shirt in several shades of red. Her hair swung loose around her face.

'You're not answering your doorbell,' she pointed out.

He smiled warily. 'I didn't think it would be you.' He hoped she hadn't come for another row. She wasn't smiling and that looked all wrong. In fact, it made him want to cheer her up. 'Would you like to come in for a cuppa?'

After a moment, she shook her head.

He waited.

Philly remained silent, staring at the sharply pointed rear wing of the car as if deep in thought. At length she said, 'Fancy a walk by the river?' Her feet, in her favourite blue basketball boots with red tartan laces, moved restlessly.

'Sounds nice,' he said, gently. 'I'll fetch my jacket.'

By the river, the still evening air was full of gnats. Kenny felt the chill that rose from the green water as the sun dodged in and out of the clouds, but Philly gave no sign of being uncomfortable. She maintained a thoughtful silence as they walked.

Kenny paced beside her. What were Philly's feelings towards him, and why had she sought him out when he'd thought their relationship in tatters?

They strode along the towpath where children fed swans and families walked dogs, past the lock, where they paused to watch a boat manoeuvring its way in between the huge iron paddles and the paddles being wound shut behind it. Then they reached the place where the tarmac path petered out to a stony, grassy and sometimes muddy track that took them on one of their favourite walks beside the fields where the brambles and cow parsley grew.

On one side of them was the town and on the other the rolling Northamptonshire countryside, the brilliant yellow of the oil-seed a prominent feature of the patchwork of fields. On the horizon could be seen the church and roofs of a village in a fold of the hills. Behind them the sprawl of the town, houses, industrial units, office blocks. When they reached a stile Philly paused and rested her arms on top to regard the countryside.

Kenny paused beside her. 'Nice view.'

Sighing, she said, 'I suppose so. But this is what I've seen all my life. The yellow fields will turn green again when they harvest, and the green fields will turn gold when the wheat and barley ripen. Then they'll all turn brown in autumn when they're ploughed, and stay that way till spring. The river will keep running. The town will keep spreading. The market will be in the centre Tuesdays, Fridays, Saturdays and occasional Sundays. People will be born here, grow up, grow old.'

'And that's not enough for you,' he said, softly, knowing what she'd brought him here to tell him.

She turned, her eyes shining with tears and lower lip trembling. 'I want to see other things. I want to see mountains, deserts, fjords, jungles and waterfalls. Skyscrapers, too, vast bridges, old buildings, quaint villages, sprawling cities.' She moved so that their elbows touched on the worn, lichen-pocked rail. Her eyes were fixed to his. 'And I want your love! I want to be with you. I want to see you every day. But it seems as if I have to sacrifice one or the other.'

She sniffed. 'I have to apologise to your Chloë, I was offish with her today and tried to blame her for talking you out of travelling with me. That eldest girl of Ed Wright's gave me a flea in my ear about it, accused me of interfering between father and daughter. She made me feel ashamed, because she was right. But whether or not I interfered out of self interest doesn't make any difference, does it? You don't want to leave Chloë and you don't want to see the wonders of the world.'

Kenny thought about skyscrapers and deserts. He rasped his chin with the pad of a thumb. 'No, I don't,' he admitted. 'But I don't agree that you have to choose between travelling and my love.' It wasn't his way to say words such as 'love' very often, and he was quite pleased to manage it without stumbling. He slid his arm around her shoulders.

'My love will go anywhere you go. Up mountains, across the sea. It'll climb to the top of a pyramid, if you take it with you. But that's the bit that's up to you. Whether you take it, and whether you keep it.'

Softly, Philly began to cry, and Kenny pulled her close. He kissed her temple, her hair, he whispered soft words of comfort. But all the time his heart leaden in his chest.

'I'll come back,' she sobbed.

'I hope that you do,' he murmured. 'I really hope you do.'

But, looking over her head at the yellow and green fields that were a familiar and dear to him as his family, he thought that someone who wanted to see fjords and jungles would more than likely find that after that there were glaciers they had missed, or mighty canyons. Always something new to see. Always somewhere fresh to go. No matter what got left behind.

Chapter Six

Ed watched Dr Farrelly shine his pencil light into Emily's eyes. Emily looked small and defenceless in the expanse of smooth white hospital bed with machines gathered around her like solemn guardian angels. He didn't think he'd experienced anything more excruciating in his life than this past week, and having to see his little girl lying unconscious.

'Slow but steady improvement,' said the doctor, quietly. His hair was short and wavy, peppered with grey hairs, and a black stethoscope looked poised to uncoil from the top pocket of his white coat. 'She's definitely more responsive. We can hope for progress in the coming days.'

'She'll come round, do you mean?' shot out Ed, hope flaring like a firework in his chest.

But the doctor was not in the business of giving guarantees. 'Well, we'll have to wait and see. We mustn't be impatient but we can be hopeful.' But at least, this time, he smiled.

Emily's eyes were sometimes open and occasionally she moved a limb. Ed tried not to look at the dressing on the left side of her head that covered the curving wound where her pony's hoof had caught her just at the edge of her riding helmet. She was sustained by a tube and monitored by a machine in the hush of the intensive care ward, as were other equally ill people around her, and Ed had begun to hear the soft beeps in his sleep. At least Emily no longer needed the ventilator.

The doctor moved on to another patient and Ed took Emily's hand. He squeezed it, and, after a moment, Emily squeezed reassuringly back. That was good, the doctor said so. Then she squeezed twice more.

He froze. Something new! Until now she'd only reacted to a squeeze from him with a single squeeze in reply. 'Emily? Darling?' But despite the urgency in Ed's voice there was no further response. Ed's heart settled back into its rightful place and he tried to quash his disappointment and talk to his daughter, as he had for so many hours, about the family and Emily's friends and the messages her teachers had sent. Perhaps Emily could hear him, that's what they said. Perhaps he was stimulating her brain.

Two hours later he woke from a maze of dreams, feeling anxious. He was hot and dizzy and it took him several seconds to realise that he'd somehow managed to fall asleep with his cheek pressed stickily against the wing of the blue vinyl hospital chair and Emily's thin hand still clasped in his.

It took him several more to comprehend that Dr Farrelly was back beside the bed with a nurse, Emily's notes in hand and that the doctor was talking to Emily. 'Hello, Emily,' he said. And. 'Hello, Emily,' again. He glanced across to Ed. 'We've got a lot of movement from her.'

Shakily, Ed climbed to his feet. He felt disoriented, as if he'd just climbed down from a whirling fairground ride.

The doctor's attention returned to his patient. 'Hello, Emily, can you squeeze my hand? Excellent, good girl. Can you poke your tongue out for me?' A pause. *'Good* girl! Wonderful. And this arm, can you give it a little wiggle?'

Another pause, but then the left arm lifted and fell again. Then rose once more, and Emily's hand went up towards her head.

'Yes, you've got a dressing on your head. You bumped it when you fell from your pony and you're in hospital now. Dad's here. Your dad's here to keep you company. Now, how about moving this leg for me?'

Emily moved the leg.

And then Emily made a noise. It wasn't a word but it was undeniably Emily's voice, and Ed felt hot tears slipping down his cheeks while a sob tore at his throat.

There had been times when he feared he'd never hear his daughter's voice again.

'That's *very* good,' the doctor approved. 'Well done, Emily.'

Then Emily turned onto her side and closed her eyes, sliding her hand under her pillow just as she did at home.

'She's gone back to sleep,' observed Dr Farrelly. 'That's fine, she'll sleep a good deal, we can't expect too much, too soon. But we can put that down as progress. Real progress.'

'This is exactly what I didn't want!' Philly heaved her rucksack into the boot of the car and flung herself into the passenger seat. Her khaki combat trousers made a foil for a yellow T-shirt with a blue and red burst of colour on the front. Her earrings, mini chandeliers of silver with purple glass, swung with every movement. 'I wanted to get the train!'

Kenny had known her too long to be moved by her exasperation. 'But as the trains aren't running because of a big power failure in Bedford, you're going to have to let me use a day's holiday to drive you there in style, aren't you?'

Philly paused, then grinned. 'Kenny, I'm sorry, I'm being an ungrateful brat. But as a first step in my grand odyssey, being chauffeured to the airport seems a bit tame!' Her voice softened and she laid a hand on his arm, her fingernails sporting jaunty pictures of palm trees. 'And I wanted to say goodbye to you at home, not at the airport in a crowd of strangers.'

He stifled a sigh as he put the car in gear and pulled away from the kerb and joked, 'We can say goodbye in the car and then I'll tip you out in the road outside the terminal doors.'

But, of course, that would mean sacrificing the last few precious minutes with her so when they finally reached the busy network of roads around the airport he swung into the dim cavern of the multi-storey car park, preparing to remain by her side for as long as her departure process allowed. He even carried her green rucksack across the footbridge and in through the door marked *Departures*, despite her vehement protests. He shared her tedious wait in the queue to check her rucksack in, hovered in the brightly lit shop while she bought two magazines and a book, and joined her for a late lunch in a fragrant coffee shop. The noisy airport hum was punctuated by echoing announcements about luggage safety and stray passengers as they talked about the market and cars and Chloë's paintings. And anything but Philly's imminent departure.

But he was aware that she was keeping one eye on the screens that charted the progress of departing aeroplanes and her flight moving its way inexorably up the list.

'BA393 to Thailand – on time,' she read out, eventually. 'I'd better go through to the departure lounge.'

'Yes.' Kenny forced a smile and climbed reluctantly to his feet. 'Got everything? Passport? Ticket? Clean hanky?' His voice caught in his throat.

Philly's bottom lip trembled suddenly as she accepted his hand to pull her up. 'Here we are saying goodbye in a crowd of strangers, overhearing the things I want to say.'

'Forget the crowd,' he muttered. 'We're the only ones that matter.'

157

She threw her arms around him, tears flooding her big blue eyes. 'I love you, Kenny Brannigan! One day I'll come home and tell you again.'

'I love you, too.' He held her close and tightly, breathing in her scent, perhaps for the last time. 'Maybe we should've said that more often while we had the chance.'

The drive home took nearly three hours. At least fifteen minutes of that was wasted queuing to get out of the airport environs, and forty more queuing through road works as he envisaged Philly sitting on a huge white aircraft while the jet engines rose to the task of catapulting her and her fellow travellers into the air. And when she landed in twelve hours' time she'd step into a new, adventuresome life full of new colours, sounds and smells. Another language would fall on her ears. Her head would fill with Bangkok, and the rolling landscape of Northamptonshire would retreat into her memory.

And so would he.

Creeping along in first gear in the blazing sun on a grey English motorway beside an endless line of cones Kenny fanned himself irritably and cast envious glances at others looking cool and comfortable in their modern cars. Much as he loved his 30 year old Beetle, it was sadly lacking in the air conditioning department. He felt like a sausage on a barbeque.

It had been a bleak day and the feeling of missing Philly seemed part of the suffocating heat that wrapped him up. He couldn't wait to get home.

But then when he was finally cutting through the familiar streets of red brick terraced houses only a few minutes from Bryant Street he thought about spending the evening by himself, perhaps turning the television on for company or trying to keep himself busy on the Corsair and home suddenly lost its appeal.

Missing Philly could only be that much harder with no one to distract his thoughts.

He had plenty of friends he could call on, he supposed, but he knew there was only one person apart from Phillipa whose company he really craved. So he drove straight past the end of Bryant Street and through town to The Avenue.

It was the first time he'd ever called for Chloë at The Old Manse without arrangement and he hoped he wouldn't be putting anybody out. But with things being as they were with poor young Emily in the fix she

159

was, he couldn't imagine that they'd be entertaining or anything.

He parked the car on the drive – an area almost big enough to hold an autojumble on, he thought – and released himself with relief from the overheated confines of the little car.

'Hello, Kenny!' Jason poked his head around one corner of the house near a big cherry tree. 'I heard you pull up on the gravel. Do you want Chloë? She's in the back garden; I'll show you.'

Quite glad to be spared the necessity of ringing the bell at the imposing front door of the house but rather wishing it had been Chloë who'd come to investigate his arrival, Kenny followed Jason around the building and out into a garden that stepped down from the house in a series of little stone walls and big lawns like something off the telly.

'Visitor, Chloë,' called Jason. 'Come and sit down, Kenny.' And Jason flung himself into one of a group of wrought iron chairs with yellow cushions.

'*Dad!*' Chloë leapt from another of the chairs even as Kenny saw with dismay that Shelly was there, too, presiding over a china teapot on a smart tiled table in the dappled shade of an apple tree. 'Did Philly get off OK?'

'Yes, she's on her way now.' He had to look away from his daughter's eyes as they brimmed with sympathy. Sympathy always made him feel worse, not better.

Giving Chloë a big hug he nodded at Shelly cautiously, not at all sure how she'd feel at him intruding on her new home and family. It felt most peculiar, and he was very conscious that in their old life together there would have been no civilised afternoon tea, no china, no apple tree, and not even any room to sit on the bit of grass that passed for a lawn – because there was normally a dismantled car on it! She had an altogether more gracious lifestyle these days.

But Shelly smiled as if delighted to see him. 'You must've smelt the tea brewing, Kenny. Chloë, would you run in and get another cup, please? Dad looks as if he could murder a drink.'

As it seemed easier to accept than to refuse, Kenny took one of the empty chairs. 'If it's no trouble.'

'Of course it isn't.'

'I hope you don't mind me calling in to see Chloë; turning up unannounced, like,' he went on, awkwardly.

161

'Not in the least. I would normally still be at work but I'm trying to finish promptly once in a while so I can spend a bit more time with the children while Ed's at the hospital so much. They're being so good, honestly.'

Kenny asked after Emily. As he listened to Shelly's reply he noted that she spoke slightly differently these days, more like Ed Wright and his friends. In many ways she was becoming more and more a stranger to him and if it wasn't for Chloë, dancing back out onto the terrace with another white china cup and saucer, he'd think that he'd dreamt them ever having been man and wife.

Watching her pouring his tea, adding milk and half a spoon of sugar without having to ask, he realised two things: it wasn't going to be too easy to whisk Chloë away on her own, as she was taking up her own cup of tea and taking up a conversation with Jason and Shelly that his arrival had evidently interrupted. And Shelly was right – he *could* murder a cuppa!

He might as well relax and enjoy a bit of company. It would take his mind off the fact that every second took Philly further away. Eight miles a minute, that was the average speed a jumbo jet cruised at, he'd read recently. From Kettering town centre to

Wellingborough's was eight miles and that's how far she'd gone while Shelly poured his tea and explained that Emily wasn't out of the woods yet.

He ached to think how far that plane would take her in nearly twelve hours.

Everyone was on their second cup of tea and explaining to Kenny the plan for a little girl called Lori to ride Emily's pony, Junk, until such time as Emily was well enough for the arrangement to be made permanent, when Melissa and Patrick stepped through the French doors. 'There you are,' exclaimed Melissa, sticking her bottom lip out and blowing her fringe off her forehead. 'Gosh, you're not drinking tea on a hot day like this, are you? Patrick, shall I get us something cold to drink? Sit down and I'll bring it out. Oh hello, Mr Brannigan,' she added, with a cool smile.

'Hello, Melissa,' responded Kenny, cautiously. He wasn't sure about Chloë's oldest stepsister and suspected her of being a bit of a madam. She'd break a few hearts before she was much older, that was for sure, so tall and pretty and with that way about her when she chose to put herself out, but he wasn't certain that Chloë hadn't had a bit of trouble with her.

They all seemed friendly enough at the moment because when Jason shouted after her, 'Bring me one!' Chloë raised her voice, too– 'And me! And biscuits, please, Melissa!'

And although Melissa called back, 'What did your last slave die of?' in a few minutes she was back with a tray of biscuits, a large jug of squash clinking with ice and sufficient glasses for everybody. And as she placed a glass in front of him she asked, 'How are you, Mr Brannigan?' as nicely as you liked.

Kenny shifted in his chair. 'I'm fine, thanks, but I'll be better if you call me Kenny like Jason does.' But he noted that Ed Wright's kids had certainly been brought up to know their manners.

Presently the children were insulting each other in the wholesale way that passed for conversation amongst teenagers, their feet propped casually on one another's chairs and he could manage a quiet word with Shelly. 'It looks as if Chloë's settling in here?' The prospect gave him a pang but of course his main priority was that his daughter was happy. If she couldn't live with him then he wanted her with Shelly, and settled.

Shelly glanced over at where their daughter was drawing cartoons of Patrick, making him gurgle with delighted laughter at her

164

ridiculous vision of his cowlick of hair and face full of freckles. 'Yes, quite well, I think. To be honest, this awful business with poor Emily has made them forget any petty squabbles. Oh, excuse me.' Delving in her bag, she pulled out her mobile phone that was calling for her attention with a discreet ring, glanced at the readout on the little screen and put it to her ear. 'Hello, Nathan!'

Shelly saw no reason to get up and move away while she answered her call from her dynamic young boss at the agency. Henson King's junior partner, Nathan. She liked Nathan. The older partners, Jack Henson and Douglas King were very nice but it was Nathan that flew through his work infecting everyone else with his energy. Working with him was like riding around on a comet, and Shelly loved it.

As usual, his tone was eager but warm. 'Sorry if I'm interrupting you with a client, Shelly.'

She laughed, looking around herself at the beautiful terraces lazing in the sunlight. 'Not this time! I need to spend some time with my family so I left at five today.'

'*Did* you?' There was a silence for several moments. 'Right. Yes. Well. So … do you mean that you won't be calling back into the agency tonight?' There was a faint note of incredulity in his voice.

Shelly smiled. Nathan probably thought of five o'clock as the middle of the day. 'Not this time,' she repeated.

'Ah. Because I need your help on Monday.'

'Of course.' Shelly began to dig through her handbag. 'Hang on while I get my diary.'

'Oh, clear your diary! We're flying up to Edinburgh on Monday to woo a potential new client – a big one! A holiday company, rather glamorous. They do a significant proportion of their business through the Internet, so your input will be invaluable. We'll get an early flight and you can expect to be wining and dining and exerting your charm for a few days. I need you to be on top form, here, Shelly! These guys could put a lot of top business Henson King's way.'

'A few days?' repeated Shelly, blankly, her heart hollowing. 'I can't go away for a few days, next week.'

Nathan paused again. Then, equally blankly, 'Why not?'

Shelly couldn't believe her ears. 'You know why not! Because my step daughter is in a coma in hospital and my husband and the other children need me here!'

Nathan became suddenly terse. 'But this is

important! This company has had a falling out with their present agency and a lucrative account is up for grabs. But we must move quickly!'

Shelly's voice rose a note. 'You must be able to see that I can't abandon my family at the moment! Emily is in *intensive care!* My family *needs me!*'

'For goodness' sake don't be so dramatic! There must be someone who can fill in for you?'

'At Henson King – yes.' Shelly was suddenly icy. 'At home – *no.*'

Nathan's voice matched hers for frostiness. 'I suppose I can't force you into showing commitment to your career. We'll talk further about this when I come back at the end of the week. That's if your *family* don't need you at the time, of course.'

Shelly wasn't one bit diverted by the note of threat in his words. 'I think we'll both have plenty to say at that meeting!' She snapped her phone shut, and found she was shaking.

Everyone was watching her in profound silence and with sympathetic expressions.

'We could probably manage for a few days, now that I'm driving,' ventured Jason. 'Between me and Melissa and Chloë we'll look after Patrick so that dad can be at the hospital and you can make your business trip.'

Chloë and Melissa smiled and nodded.

Trying to overcome anger at Nathan's highhanded dismissal of the seriousness of her family situation, Shelly slid her phone back into her bag with a weak smile. 'Thank you, but I wouldn't leave you all at this time.'

'Good for you!' said Kenny.

Shelly felt her nails curling into her palms. Kenny's approbation didn't soothe her at all! He meant well, but it rankled that none of her hard won career success had ever gained his approval – it took her to abandon her job before she got that!

But her real anger was directed at Nathan because it was the first time ever that she had shown less than 100% commitment to the agency and Nathan's lack of sympathy, in the circumstances, was just unforgivable. She deserved better than that.

Chloë had been hugging a secret to herself all day. And it was mega that her father had turned up so unexpectedly because now she could tell her news to both her parents at once!

She still could scarcely believe in her fantastic secret and had spent the walk home from school reliving every moment of receiv-

168

ing the news. Mrs Meredith had come to find her in her maths class and asked Mr Smith if she could 'borrow' Chloë Brannigan for ten minutes. When, beaming like a lighthouse she'd given Chloë the astonishing news Chloë had thought she'd explode with joy.

'Are you sure it's me?'

'Of course I'm sure! And now I have to take you along to Mrs Somers, to receive her congratulations!' she'd added. 'We're all so proud that a student from Norman's Wood Community College could achieve something like this!' Chloë had followed her to the headteacher's office in a daze.

And if she didn't tell somebody else about it, soon, she'd reach explosion pitch again.

Shelly having the uncharacteristic spat with her boss made Chloë's heart sink, thinking that she might have to put her great announcement aside for just a little longer. But when her father began to look at his watch and talk about going home for dinner she knew that this was the time.

Apart from a natural desire to pass on the news to her parents together instead of in turn, as was normally the case, once Ed got home the talk would all, quite naturally, be about Emily. And as with Jason passing his driving test, Chloë was well aware that vaunting good news at the wrong time could seem callous.

'I've had some good news.' She waited to make certain she had her parents' attention, even though Shelly was still flushed and glittery eyed with anger, then took a deep breath. 'Last term Mrs Meredith, the head of the art department, sent in work by three students to a schools' art competition run by some arts council – and I've just heard that I'm the regional winner!'

Jason was the first to break the startled silence. 'That's really cool!' And he slapped her on the back.

'Wicked!' agreed Patrick. 'Are you going to be famous? And rich?'

'Brilliant!' said Melissa. 'Good one.'

Her parents seemed to come to life then and took it in turns to embrace her with cries of 'Well *done!*' and 'I'm so proud of you!'

'I won't be famous but I'm going to be in the local paper.' Chloë felt herself going redder and redder with excitement. 'A photographer's coming to the school on Monday morning.'

'But what have you won?' demanded Patrick.

Chloë beamed. 'A whole load of art equipment for the school, and some for me.'

Melissa was frowning. 'You said you're the regional winner. That suggests that there are other winners from other regions. What happens next?'

Chloë could scarcely sit still in her seat. 'There's going to be an exhibition of the work of all the regional winners in London. And then *that's* going to be judged, and three people selected for special workshops in London, on Saturdays, two a month for at least a year. It's a kind of scholarship. Those who have progressed well by the end of the year will get a mentor, if they'd like one – as if they wouldn't! – and help approaching art schools and with their portfolios and everything! It would be fantastic!'

'Wow!' breathed Patrick. 'Are we allowed to go and see the exhibition in London?'

'Yes, anybody can.'

She gazed around, self-conscious suddenly at the silence and the awestruck expressions. 'But I don't suppose I'll win one of those places. I'm the youngest person in it. Oh, wow, Mum! Don't cry!'

Smiling through her tears, Shelly blotted beneath her eyes with the back of her hand. 'I can't help it, darling, I'm just so proud!' She turned impulsively to Kenny. 'Why don't you stay and eat with us? It can be a celebration for Chloë!'

'Oh, I don't know!' objected Kenny. 'Ed might not like to come home and–'

'Nonsense!' Shelly got to her feet. 'There's a huge casserole in the oven, enough for all of us, and there's no telling when, or even if, Ed will be home to eat his. We must celebrate with Chloë, it's such a huge day for her!' She loaded the tray with empty cups and glasses and swept off towards the house with Jason and Melissa heeding the call of homework and following on, Patrick roaring off in front in an imitation of a jet fighter.

Chloe looked at Kenny.

Kenny looked back at her.

'Seems a bit funny.' He rubbed the tip of his nose with the flat of his hand as he did when he was uneasy.

'Yes.' Chloë bit her lip, watching her father fidget uncomfortably. On the one hand she sympathised. A social gathering weren't really his thing and she wasn't at all surprised if a gathering in Ed's house was even less appealing than any other. But, on the other hand, it would be a nicer celebration for her if he stayed...

He reached for her hand and squeezed it hard. 'But I don't want to miss your celebration, Chloë! I just can't tell you how

172

proud! My daughter in a London exhibition!' His voice dried up.

She jumped to her feet. 'It'll only be an hour, Dad. Ed won't mind, he's invited you in for drinks before. He probably won't even turn up until late.' She used their clasped hands to heave him out of his chair. 'Come and drink to my success in lemonade!'

Wearily, Ed let his car roll to a halt on the gravel. Next to Shelly's red car and Jason's white one was a pale blue Beetle with the windows open. He had no trouble recognising the vehicle as one that Kenny drove; the chrome gleamed under the lights and the bodywork showed no blemish. He sighed. He quite liked Kenny and had certainly come to respect him for his work ethic and the priority he gave to his daughter. But Ed had had a long day and didn't feel like being sociable.

He let his head tip back on the rest. He was so tired. Emily was making progress and had moved several more times throughout the day, most of the time responding to requests to move her limbs. But she'd gone no further forward than that and Ed was so disappointed that he could cry. He was an intelligent man and he *knew* that Emily wasn't going to just sit up and ask for breakfast. The doctor had told him that there was really no formula for a patient recovering from head trauma. He couldn't guess what would come next except there would be no moment of drama. No instant recovery. No one moment of unspeakable relief.

But that hadn't stopped Ed hoping.

Indoors, he had only to follow his ears to seek out the other occupants of the house. Loud chatter and laughter drew him across the parquet hall floor and past the imposing oak staircase through to the back of the house. And there they all were, sitting around the kitchen table with empty plates stacked on the work surface, just digging in to a plateful of Barbara's delicious chocolate brownies.

Kenny, who had his back to the door, for some reason was making an awkward little speech about being proud of Chloë and raising his glass first to Chloë and then to Shelly, 'To our daughter!' Shelly was raising her glass in return, her eyes shining as they rested on the man she used to be married to, when she noticed Ed.

She put down her glass. 'Hello, darling! Your dinner's keeping warm, shall I put it out for you? We've been having a little celebration!'

'Really.' He stared around the table. Kenny, he noticed, was looking uncomfortable. 'What are *you* celebrating?' He knew his voice was cold and quite probably sarcastic. He saw Shelly's face fall and her lips part uncertainly.

It was Kenny who filled the silence. 'Chloë's the regional winner of a big schools art competition. Her work's going to London to be judged and she might win a kind of scholarship.'

Ed's lips felt stiff as he said, 'Congratulations, Chloë. I'm sorry I couldn't be here to share your celebration.'

Chloë reddened, saying uneasily, 'We didn't know how late you'd be or we would've waited. Sometimes you're very late.'

'Yes. Pity I couldn't have been included.' Ed stalked to the aga and grabbed a cloth to use to take out his plate. He found himself a place at the table and clean cutlery and sat down to his meal. Chicken casserole and dumplings, one of his favourite, but tonight it might as well have been balls of wool. Still, he put the first forkful to his mouth.

He knew everyone was watching him, understanding that he was upset but not entirely understanding why. He knew he was being childish and unreasonable; it wasn't normally in him to take a pet because he'd been left out. Chloë was quite right about him getting home late – sometimes it was past eleven at night and he could scarcely expect them to wait their dinner till then, celebration or not.

But anger and misery was growing inside him like a black canker, he was so scared for Emily and he knew there was nothing anybody could do for her more than was being done. And here was Kenny holding a celebration for *his* daughter at Ed's table, when Ed's own little girl lay in intensive care having her limbs moved for her by a physiotherapist and doctors and nurses speaking to her as if she could hear, although she gave little sign of doing so. It did him no credit, but he'd felt jealous when he'd walked in and seen Kenny, Chloë and Shelly so joyful, and his own selection of the family joining in so happily.

And Shelly had been looking at Kenny with such affection…

Kenny was the first to speak. 'How is Emily?'

Ed forced another mouthful down. 'She's more responsive, thank you.'

The others all leapt in with eager questions about what *more responsive* meant, but it was Kenny's quiet voice that Ed heard. 'You must be beside yourself.'

Ed felt his eyes boil with tears. 'Yes,' he agreed, hoarsely.

Later, upstairs, Shelly got ready for bed slowly, brushing her hair and removing her make-up, applying the exclusive moisturiser that she now used without thought for the expense.

Ed already lay under the sheets with the sprigged satin cover, staring at the ceiling.

'Did something awful happen today? At the hospital?'

He blinked. 'Everything at the hospital is awful.'

Shelly hesitated. 'But you've been particularly quiet this evening.'

'I've talked myself hoarse with Emily all day.'

Shelly crossed the soft cream wool carpet and slid into bed beside him. She lay an arm lightly on his chest. 'You didn't like Kenny being here, did you?'

He shrugged. 'I've nothing against Kenny.'

But Shelly pressed the point, knowing that it was important. 'So why were you so hostile?'

'Was I?' His gaze moved about the ceiling

as if he might find answers there. 'It was a little difficult for me to watch you all being so happy, in the circumstances. And for you two to be congratulating yourselves on your wonderful daughter…'

Shelly stroked his cheek. He hadn't shaved since morning and it was rough beneath her fingertips. 'It's not like you to be so sour over the good fortune of others, darling. Poor Emily has been ill for over a week and you haven't come home in a filthy mood until today.'

With a long sigh, Ed slung his arm across his eyes. 'The doctor said some things to me. He said that head injury happens to whole families, not just the patient. I should be prepared for it to affect us all – as if I hadn't worked that one out already! And he said that head injuries can make a person different – not necessarily less capable, but changed. But I don't want Em to be *different!* I want her back as she was! I don't want her to "behave in confusing and unfamiliar ways", as he called it! Shelly, I've been wishing so hard for her to come round.'

He dragged his arm away and turned blindly towards her for comfort. 'But what if she's a stranger when she does?'

Chapter Seven

'We mustn't expect too much,' Ed said. 'She's going to need a lot of peace and quiet.'

His family shook their heads with a solemnity belied by their hopeful faces.

'We'll need to be understanding,' nodded Jason.

'No pressure,' contributed Melissa.

'She's still getting headaches.' Chloë patted Ed's hand.

Patrick grinned. 'I'm not allowed to run around screaming. Nor are my friends. But it'll still be nice to have Em back! Do we *really* have to go to school while you go and fetch her from the hospital. You could write a note–'

'We'd be dead quiet!' Jason shot in.

Melissa threw back her hair. 'Yes, Dad – can't we stay? It seems wrong for Em to come back to an empty house–'

Ed had to swallow a lump in his throat at their earnest expressions before he spoke. 'Sorry, kids. I know you all want to welcome Emily, but we've got to think what's best for her – and that will be for her to be home and settled before she has to cope with chit chat. I won't get her here until mid-afternoon anyway, so she'll just have a nice hour or so to get used to the place before you hordes arrive.'

The children pulled faces and exchanged mutinous glances but, one by one, picked up their school things and shuffled out of the kitchen. Jason could be heard plotting even before he was out of earshot. 'We'll take my car, Melissa, it's quicker to get home than on the school bus. Chloë, you're going to fetch Patrick, aren't you?'

'Yes, they've given me permission to leave quarter of an hour early. We'll all get home about the same time.'

Patrick groaned. 'I'm sure Em wouldn't mind if we were here...'

Ed watched them go, good natured Jason who Ed would like to take for a haircut; willowy, collected Melissa; scatty, freckled Patrick with his enormous grin. They were good children. Their yearning to see their sister home again did them credit and it would have been lovely to organise a big welcome for Emily. But that, according to the medical staff, was exactly what *shouldn't* happen.

'You need to go very gently with her,' the doctors and nurses warned. 'She needs to be kept away from excitement. Let her find her feet slowly. A safe, peaceful environment is a must at first.'

Whereas his children's ideas went more with banners, balloons and an uproarious dinner!

Across the table sat his wife, her hair fair and glossy on her shoulders. She had added nothing to the conversation but her eyes were fixed on him with concern. She smiled. 'The children are so excited!'

He reached across for her hand. 'I know, Shelly! That's the trouble!'

'And what about me? Shall I keep you company until it's time to fetch her? I think time might drag for you here alone.'

'Oh, you'll want to go to work,' he said, surprised. 'I know they're being very good about you working nine-to-five just now but the agency won't want you to miss any time you don't have to. Anyway, I must go into the office this morning, there are things to arrange. After lunch I'll get along to the hospital.'

'OK, darling.' Shelly picked up her bag and brushed crumbs from her clothes. The dark pink suit teamed well with French navy shoes and bag each sporting one pink button to match the suit exactly. Ed thought she looked a million dollars. 'I'll see you after work. I hope everything goes well with Em.' She kissed him, glanced at her watch, and left.

The house was suddenly silent. Ed looked around at the dishes stacked by the dishwasher and the few things left on the table. In ten minutes Barbara would arrive and whisk through a clear up of the room. Later in the day, she would make fragrant lasagne with extra cheese and garlic bread for dinner – Emily's favourite, she'd reminded him. And he'd be very surprised if chocolate mousse didn't make an appearance, too. Everybody wanted Emily home and each chose their particular method of showing it.

And nobody wanted her home more than Ed himself!

He helped himself to the last of the coffee and carried it with him upstairs to make one final – unnecessary – check that Emily's room was ready for her. Not a pink and fluffy room as many girls her age might have chosen but plain cream walls the better to display her collection of horse pictures and riding heroes. He tried not to look at the hook where her riding helmet normally hung. Then he shrugged into his jacket, adjusted his tie, and left for the office. He had an important meeting this morning.

He chose to walk through the Avenue Windows workshop this morning, rather than taking the side door that would lead him directly to the offices. A big, purpose built unit with a lofty roof, the workshop was full of the clatter and conversation of industry and the sharp smell of plastic. As he wandered between the work benches members of his staff looked up, smiled, nodded, offered him, "Morning!' or, 'All right?' Some wore safety glasses and ear defenders. They worked on window frames, doors and frames, double-glazed units, leaded and stained glass. The coffee machine gurgled and the radio played.

It was all as familiar and dear to him as his own house.

He glanced into the Sales Office where phone conversations were already underway on smart black headsets and computer screens shone back at him through the glass. Waving at Wynne in Accounts and Alan on Payroll, he turned to climb the stairs up to his own office with the black leather chairs and the big mahogany desk.

Cliff and Rod, his right hand men, were waiting for him, pads and pens on the desk before them.

''Morning,' he said, closing the door and crossing to the largest chair behind the desk. He put down his briefcase and hung up his jacket, then looked at his senior staff – his friends – and smiled. 'Firstly, I want to thank you both for all the extra work you've put in since Emily was hurt. I can't tell you what a relief it was not to have to worry about the factory. To know it was safe in your hands.'

'She's getting better, that's the main thing,' said Cliff.

Ed gazed keenly at the two, men who'd worked their way up from bench work and knew as much about the business as Ed himself. Cliff, with the lugubrious expression that hid a puckish sense of humour and Rod who never seemed to take his hands out of his pockets but somehow got everything done that he was meant to.

'I agree. And the purpose of this morning's meeting,' Ed continued, trying to smile, 'is to discuss how to proceed from here. To give you what you need to continue to share my job. Because Emily is coming home today and somebody has to stay at home with her for the next weeks or even months. And that somebody is going to be me.'

Across town, in another office, Shelly was having a thoroughly unpleasant time.

Douglas King was normally approachable enough but today Shelly was finding him intransigent.

'I've given one hundred per cent to the agency,' she pointed out, hoping her voice wouldn't waver and betray her hurt and anger.

Douglas nodded gently, smoothing back his hair, winged with grey now. 'Nobody's disputing that, Shelly.'

'Don't I deserve a little latitude?'

'Yes – and I think we've bent over backwards to give it to you. I think I'm correct in saying that you're now able to leave your duties promptly at the end of the day to be with your family?'

'Yes, *but*–'

'And we've agreed that you must take any personal time that you need in the event of further crisis?'

Shelly clenched her hands on the arms of the chair in frustration. Her heart was pattering as fast as the rain on the window outside and her face was hot. She must keep calm. Disguise her fury so that she could put her point clearly and logically.

'But, Douglas, this has been accomplished

by relieving me of my client list, which strips me of my seniority, essentially, and makes me a glorified assistant! You've left me with no real work to do. I've worked hard for the agency, and the list of clients I've built up is profitable.'

Douglas spread his hands in a *What can be done?* gesture. 'Nobody disputes that you have been an asset to the agency. But you must be the first to admit, Shelly, that success like that demands long hours and trips away from home. When you told us that you were no longer able to undertake those things because of serious domestic problems, we simply rearranged the work that needed to be done in a way that would accommodate those needs.'

Her heart thumped harder. 'Nathan began this! It was *one trip!* He knew about my stepdaughter and asked me to be available for a trip at a totally inappropriate moment!'

For the first time Douglas looked impatient. He let her see him glancing at the chrome clock on the matt grey wall. 'Shelly, if I asked you to hurry home and pack a bag and accompany me this afternoon to a client in Cornwall for a week, would you come?'

Shelly felt herself become still. Her heart stopped its hammering and sank slowly down into her shoes as she saw the trap she was about to plummet into. 'Emily's coming home *today*, but any other time…'

He smiled, smoothly. 'Quite. So I think you'll agree there's little we can do but arrange tasks for you that allow for your family commitments.' Douglas said nothing further. He merely kept his hazel eyes fixed upon her as she struggled for a defence and, eventually, rose and left the room, resisting the temptation to slam the door behind her like a child in a tantrum.

Inside her head, though, as she paced over the blue carpet of the corridor, past the prints of modern art, she raged, *It's not fair! It's not!* She gained the privacy of her own office and sat down carefully at her computer. It wasn't fair, and everyone in the agency knew it.

This office was an empty status symbol now that she was filling her time supporting others who had their own clients. While newly ensconced just outside Nathan's office was a young man in a dark suit and he would gladly work till midnight every evening if Nathan requested it, and probably had a sponge bag permanently packed in is briefcase lest he were ever asked to undertake a quick trip to the moon.

Under Nathan's supervision, he was looking after Shelly's clients.

And all this because Shelly had upset Nathan, and anybody who upset Nathan tended to have a bumpy ride thereafter. It wasn't just that she'd refused to go to Scotland with him. It was because when they'd had the opportunity to discuss the matter a week later she had not only failed to apologise for her unprecedented decision not to drop everything and run for the airport but also pointed out to Nathan that some things were more important than the agency – and her family was one of them.

Chloë felt as if she could dance along the school corridors. She wanted to spread her arms, close her eyes, tilt back her head and pirouette with joy.

She was the regional finalist chosen by the arts council to have her work *on exhibition in London* – and she might even have a chance at workshops with professional artists and being mentored right into a good art school! Getting into a good art school was her major ambition. The right qualifications from the right school would be the key to her future.

And now, bliss on bliss, Mrs Meredith had more good news for her!

'The school has decided to put on a trip to go to the London exhibition to see your work on show with all the other finalists. Myself and Mrs Somers will be on the coach with you – and I believe several other members of staff. I'm going to put a notice on the board and in the registers of all the year 10, 11 and 12 groups. I think the trip will fill up in no time!'

Chloë's voice emerged as a squeak. 'Really? Do you think enough people will be interested?'

Mrs Meredith hugged herself into her out of shape blue cardigan and beamed. 'I *do* think so! One of our students doing so well in a nationwide competition doesn't happen every day, you know! You will have visited the exhibition by then, of course, with your family, by special invitation with all the other exhibitors. Are Mum and Dad excited?'

Chloë smiled shyly. 'I'm just hanging on for a day or two. My stepsister comes out of hospital today.'

Ed went alone to the hospital to collect Emily.

That was what he'd wanted. All the children and Shelly had offered – even pleaded to accompany him but he knew that Emily

189

would cope best with just her father.

She shared a cheery yellow room with one other little girl, now: Richenda. Emily's guardian angel machines had been left behind in the intensive care unit and she could've had a room to herself, but Ed agreed with the hospital that it might have been lonely for her.

But when Ed knocked and walked in Emily was alone. Richenda had gone to the coffee shop with her family.

Emily sat in a chair that looked too big for her, gazing vaguely at the television. But she looked up and smiled as he entered. She was wearing a cardigan buttoned right up to her chin so he knew she hadn't managed the buttons herself; she would never have voluntarily done up that hated top button. Buttons were one of the few things that she still couldn't do. And laces. Fine motor function, the occupational therapist called it, and declared that any lack could be sorted out when Emily was an outpatient.

'So!' began Ed, heartily. 'Home today!'

'Yes.' Emily smiled, but there was a pucker of anxiety above her eyes.

Ed had been warned about this. Patients who had been kept in hospital for quite short periods found it strange leaving the environment where they'd felt so safe and where everything revolved around them. And children who had been seriously ill were the worst of all. It took almost no time for them to think of their hospital room as 'home'.

'Nothing to worry about, darling.' Ed took Emily's hand gently. 'We'll just get your case packed and then say goodbye to everybody, shall we?' That was something else he'd learnt. Some parents just whisked the child away from the people she'd had daily contact with and the child could then feel grief at not having gone through a proper leave taking from somebody they'd grown to like.

That was something Ed could relate to. He'd just taken leave of Avenue Windows and everybody who worked there for he didn't know how long, and all his relief and pleasure at Emily coming home couldn't quite override the hollow feeling that told him he missed them already. In the last couple of weeks he'd made it into the office for part of each day and the routine had comforted him, distracted him from his worries.

'You've brought a big case.' Emily spoke carefully. Her speech was still slightly thick and slow.

'I wanted to make sure I could get all your clothes in.'

The packing was soon done, accompanied by a few feeble jokes from him about leaving the laundry for the doctor to do. And soon they were walking along the corridors to seek out Nurse Alison and Nurse Nita, children Emily had made friends with in the day room and lastly Richenda in the coffee shop. The girls hugged awkwardly. Richenda's family wished Emily a speedy recovery.

Emily seemed to have grown in the last few weeks. She walked quietly beside Ed with only a small limp. She would probably appear almost as usual to the casual observer, especially as she wore her hair in bunches so that the shaved patches didn't show. Anyone who knew her better, of course, would see that she was missing her permanent air of exasperation and slight bossiness.

'Ready now?' asked Ed, when the last goodbye had been said and they returned to her room.

Emily nodded.

He lifted the case and slipped his free arm around her slight shoulders. 'You'll be back here on Monday for your appointments and you'll see Richenda and everybody then, OK?'

She managed a tiny smile at that. Ed hoped against hope that by the time Monday came around she would have settled at home.

A nurse came in to see to the written formalities and confirmed appointments with the doctor, the occupational therapist and the physiotherapist. 'We'll miss you,' she said to Emily.

Emily nodded.

'You'll come and see us?'

'Monday.'

'So soon? That'll be lovely. You try and remember.'

Emily nodded again. Her memory was haphazard at the moment. Sometimes she got halfway along the corridor then couldn't remember what she'd set out for. She could remember nothing about the accident at all. In fact, at one time she'd forgotten that her father and Shelly had married and thought they were still waiting for the wedding day to come. When Melissa reminded her, Emily said, frankly, 'Good! I thought I still had to wear that horrible dress!' Everyone had laughed.

But to Ed it was bittersweet. A glimpse of Emily's old spirit – but the old Emily would not have been so blunt in front of Shelly, who had chosen the dress. Still, the counsellor he'd spoken to had told him that a sense of humour would help enormously as

Emily progressed and so it was better that he joined in the laughter.

At home, Emily glanced around with an unfathomable expression. She looked white and weary, and Ed realised why the nurse had been so firm that she travel across the car park in a wheelchair. Her trip home had worn her out. Suddenly her face cleared. 'Can I watch television?'

'Of course you can. In the sitting room?'

Emily nodded and set off across the hall, pushing off her shoes clumsily at the entrance to the room. In seconds she was settled in the corner of a sofa with the remote control in her hand. Cheered by this initiative, Ed went to the kitchen to get her a drink of squash and a little cake that Barbara had taken out of the oven half an hour before.

When he got back, Emily was asleep, the remote control still in her hand, cartoons cavorting unheeded across the screen.

The other children arrived in pairs. First the eldest, Jason and Melissa, whispering questions at Ed, frowning their concern as Emily slumbered peacefully. Then Chloë brought Patrick home, hissing at him in the hallway, 'Remember! Quiet!'

Obligingly, Patrick performed an exaggerated tiptoe into the sitting room. But then espied his sister and exclaimed at the top of his voice, 'Oh no! She's *asleep!*'

A chorus of shushes didn't prevent Emily from waking at the noise. She gazed at her little brother and smiled. ''Lo, Patty!'

'Hello Em! If you're not watching this girly rubbish on the telly, I've got a new Spiderman DVD, shall we watch that? Budge your legs up, please.'

Emily obligingly curled her legs to allow her Patrick space to flop among the cushions. Melissa, Chloë and Jason took the other sofa and settled down to keep the younger ones company, discussing their day and Spiderman's acrobatics simultaneously.

Whether it was her nap or the undemanding company of her siblings, Em looked much brighter, even joining in the conversation from time to time.

Ed felt safe in retiring to the study with a cup of coffee and the paper. But instead of reading he found himself listening to the voices from the other room, smiling each time he heard Emily's.

And when Shelly came in just after five he hurried out into the hall to greet her with the biggest smile he'd managed in weeks, and a huge hug to welcome her home.

Dear Kenny,
  Sawadee krup! (Greetings!) I still love Bang-
kok! Everyone is friendly and I love the seafood.
Visited the Temple of the Emerald Buddha, been
on a river trip and watched beautiful Thai danc-
ing. Inspirational! Wonderful jewellery in the
shops and markets, too. Fabby colours. Miss you.
Some really old cars here – you'd love it! Moving
upriver tomorrow. Will send new address.
  And, very small and tucked in the corner
because she'd run out of room: *Love*
PhillyXXX
  The picture was of a temple – at least that's
what Kenny thought. Some pretty building,
anyway, with a series of roofs like skirts being
held up at the corners. He turned back to the
writing, though he'd read it a dozen times
since he'd arrived home from work and
found it waiting. It was the third card since
she'd left. There had been a letter, too, telling
him all about her hotel and that she'd got a
job part-time there working in the gift shop.
She'd met a young couple from Wales who
had been in Bangkok for almost a year and
given her loads of information about where
to go or where to avoid.
  Every time she wrote she said she missed

196

him and that he'd love Bangkok. He loved something that was *in* Bangkok, that was for sure!

He pinned the brightly coloured card on the corkboard in the kitchen. He'd bought the board specially. It might be a long time before Philly came home again. Therefore, there might be a lot of cards.

He turned the radio on to a classic gold channel while he made himself a meal. It wasn't that he minded the quiet, precisely. He'd lived alone for years. But now there was no prospect of chatty, laughing Philly to come and share his evenings with him, the quiet seemed quieter than it had before.

He ate his meal with the paper propped against the sauce bottle and was washing up when the doorbell rang. He paused, but then heard the scrape of the key in the lock so knew it was Chloë. She had her own key but always pressed the bell before using it.

'Hi, Dad!' His daughter bounced in as if she had springs in her trainers, her glossy hair swinging about her happy shining face.

'Someone's full of it,' he teased, with a grin. 'Won the pools?'

She snatched up a tea towel and began to dry the few pots on the draining board. 'I've had a lovely day! Emily came home. She's quiet and sleepy, but she's getting better all the time. You should see the relief on Ed's face!'

Kenny nodded, sombrely. 'Bound to have cut him up, these last few weeks. Glad Emily's making progress.'

'But that's not all!' Chloë's eyes were shining. 'I've had an invitation to the exhibition – the one I'm in! For me and my family. A celebration and a private viewing! Can you come, Dad? It's a Friday – have you got a day's holiday left? We can go on the train, it's only an hour, I know you don't like London much and you might have to wear your suit but–'

'Whoa!' Laughing, Kenny held both his soapy hands in the air in a gesture of submission. 'Of course I'll come! You try and stop me! I shall be at the head of the queue for your autograph, shouting, "Look! There's Chloë Brannigan, the famous artist!" And the paparazzi will chase you for your photo.'

She giggled and flicked him with the tea towel. 'Don't take the mickey!'

Having Chloë to spend the evening did Kenny good. She laughed and chattered and exclaimed over Philly's cards. They looked up Bangkok together – for about the fifth time – in a big atlas that Kenny had bought from the book stall on the market. They pored over the pictures of skyscrapers and highways and the beautiful dancers, their headdresses not unlike one of the golden roofs of Chakri Maha Prasat, The Grand Palace. There were statues, gardens, trains and little three-wheeled motor taxis called Tuk Tuks...

'It looks an amazing place,' breathed Chloë. 'Look at those colours! So much gold and green and red. It's beautiful.'

'And Philly says it's friendly enough.'

Chloë giggled. 'Can you imagine anyone not being friendly to Philly? She just beams all over her face and everybody beams back at her.'

Kenny shut the atlas with a slap. 'I don't know about that. I've been on the receiving end when she's been feeling unfriendly, and she's pretty good at that, too!'

With Emily's return home an odd stage in Ed's life began, a stage for which there was little training. He'd never lived life so slowly or had to be so patient.

Weekdays, when everyone else had left the house, were strangest. In the quiet period just after eight in the morning he would talk about business to Cliff and Rod on the telephone, and that was the nearest he got to normality. Emily generally woke about half-past nine and took a while eating breakfast, washing and dressing. But she was quite alert at that sort of time and they would do some form of therapy, perhaps playing a simple game or looking through a book.

Ed would make himself relax and just let Emily go at her own pace. He learnt never to try and carry on once Emily's attention wandered and he remembered how to answer the same question three times, just like when the children were toddlers.

After lunch, normally taken in the sunny kitchen with Barbara, Emily would invariably fall asleep on the sofa in front of the television, and Ed could settle down in front of the computer in the study and answer e-mails, or talk again to Cliff or Rod at the factory by phone. Occasionally one of them would call round for discussions or with things for him to sign.

And whilst he appreciated Cliff's and Rod's willingness to perform above their usual level he couldn't help feeling frustrated that his role in his own business had dwindled so dramatically.

Then Emily would wake and he'd find something else to do with her designed to stimulate her mind.

One of the most useful was to look through the family photograph albums together. This served the dual purpose of identifying people that Emily was no longer sure of and reawakening memories of past birthdays or holidays that seemed presently to have disappeared.

He learnt quickly that the name of the person she was looking at was enough information to give her. If he burdened her with labels such as cousin or aunt she became confused.

One day he took her down to the carp pond at the bottom of the garden to enjoy the fresh air as they turned the shiny pages. It was a relief to him that she'd been able to identify her mother from a photograph without having to be reminded. 'That's Mum.'

'That's right, darling! Well done! And that's Patrick with her, when he was tiny.' Ed smiled at the picture of Annabelle grinning into the camera, a baby on her hip.

Emily stared for a few moments. She rubbed her eyes as she'd begun to do when something was bothering her. 'Do you know if I used to be able to remember Mum before the accident?'

Ed didn't immediately understand. 'Oh, I think so! You *still* remember her! You've just pointed her out to me, haven't you?'

'No. I only remember the photos,' said Emily quietly. She turned away.

Beside her, Ed closed the album slowly, then stared bleakly at the pond that used to give Annabelle so much pleasure. 'She used to love to stand on the bridge here and watch the fish. You used to stand with her, and she'd hold your hand to keep you safe.'

'Yes!' Emily turned suddenly, her face ablaze with pleasure. 'I *do* remember! I remember feeding the fish with her from the bridge!'

Squeezing his daughter's hand, Ed found suddenly that he couldn't speak. Annabelle had been a serene, sunny, motherly person and Emily not remembering her for an instant had shaken him badly. Memories were almost all they had of her.

'Hello, you two! I wondered where you were hiding!' Chloë jumped down the steps. She carried a pad under her arm and a pencil tucked between her fingers. She halted when she saw their faces, her eyes flicking between the two.

Then she smiled. 'Emily, would you like to help me design a thank you card for everyone at the hospital? We can draw it here and then fix it to some silver card I have upstairs.'

'Great!' Emily brightened immediately.

Ed got to his feet. 'Have my place, Chloë.'

She glanced at him again. 'Mum's just come home.'

He glanced at his stepdaughter. 'I'll have a chat with her then, while you're drawing with Emily, shall I?'

'Yes, Em'll be fine.' Chloë smiled back.

He found Shelly in their bedroom. She had just changed out of her working clothes and into jeans and a caramel coloured top that suited her creamy colouring. It was still a novelty that she could get home so promptly and, on days like today, a relief. He gathered her in his arms and rested his head on hers, drawing comfort from her presence. 'I don't think I'm cut out to be a carer,' he mumbled.

Her arms tightened around him. 'But you're doing wonderfully!'

'I'm not doing wonderfully. I'm bumbling my way through. I'm used to being good at my job but I don't think I'm very good at this one! And it can be so painful.' He told her about Emily thinking she'd lost her memories of her mother. 'I felt so helpless! Thankfully, she dredged up a memory just as I felt I would weep for her, and your Chloë came along and rescued me. She seems to sense when people need a helping hand. What other people need from her. I wish I had the same talent!'

He heaved an enormous sigh. 'If Annabelle was here she would've looked after Emily–' He halted, and groaned. 'I'm sorry if that sounded completely insensitive! It's just that I'm finding things so difficult!'

But Shelly showed understanding. 'It's quite natural that you should miss Annabelle, you know. And especially now. I don't expect you to forget her. She was the mother of your children and she sounds like a wonderful person.'

He felt his eyes burn. 'But I want you to know that I'm very happy with you. And you've been brilliant all through Emily's illness.'

She kissed his chin, which was probably as far up his face as she could reach. 'Do you think that we ought to be looking for a nurse to–'

'No!' He cut her off. 'I'm not going to have a stranger come and look after Emily while I go back to my desk! I might not be finding my new role very easy but if there's one thing that all this has taught me, it's that there are some things more important than money. And Emily is one of them!'

Shelly patted his chest. 'You're right. I've been thinking along much the same lines. I think I might leave my job, Ed.'

Chapter Eight

'What did you just say?' Nathan stared at Shelly. His lips were set but in the eyes behind his small and trendy glasses Shelly detected shock.

'I'm leaving Henson King, Nathan,' she repeated. She tapped a long white envelope she'd placed neatly on the desk before him. 'This is my resignation.'

He glanced at the envelope. 'And this is because…?'

Shelly's heart gave a patter of irritation. As if he didn't know! 'And this is because,' she repeated, 'my family commitments mean I can't give the agency all it wants from me. Apparently, the only use I am at present is as an assistant to others – as Ross, a young man with half my qualifications and none of my experience, can handle my client list.'

Nathan fiddled with the corner of the envelope. 'I see.' He frowned. 'What will you do next?'

'Whatever I want, I suppose!'

His eyes rose to meet hers. 'You know that your resignation isn't what *I* want.'

She let her eyebrows lift, disbelievingly. 'I don't know anything of the kind. Since I "let the agency down" during the critical illness of my stepdaughter you have made a point of demonstrating just how easily the agency can do without my input.'

Nathan flushed. Then sighed. 'Sit down a minute, let's talk this over.' And then, when Shelly remained on her feet, 'Please, Shelly.'

Reluctantly, she took a seat and he went over to a coffee jug on a hotplate on a low table and poured coffee into two china mugs. She was slightly surprised to see that he knew she took half a spoon of sugar and a lot of milk. He hadn't exactly made a habit of making coffee for her.

Dropping back into his leather chair, he sighed. 'I feel I may have contributed to mismanaging this episode.'

'I have no doubt about it.'

For the first time, he smiled. A proper smile, his eyes shining. 'Good old Shelly – always direct! But it's obvious that I need to make clear what I thought you knew perfectly well: you're a valued member of this agency, and I don't want to lose you.'

Anger and indignation burnt her face scarlet. She fought to keep her voice from shaking. 'Then you shouldn't have treated me so shabbily. I used to think you were my friend, not just my boss, Nathan. But friends don't turn on people when they need help. They don't look at a painful situation and make it worse! You obviously didn't appreciate my blunt protest at being asked to work away from home at no notice when Emily was so ill. Instead of allocating me Ross to help me over these difficult weeks to repay my past loyalty, you punished me by effectively giving my job to him – an inexperienced junior. Now you're trying to retrieve the situation by refusing my resignation. Well thanks, but no thanks, Nathan.'

Silence rang around the room.

Nathan slit open and read Shelly's letter. 'All right,' he said, eventually. 'You have a right to be angry. The agency took a line that, on reflection, was not sympathetic. That was my fault and I apologise. You're right that I resented your bluntness. I don't have children of my own and possibly underestimated the effect the little girl's accident had on you.'

It was the nearest Nathan would come to a climb down. Shelly rubbed her temples.

'Thank you, I suppose.'

His eyes brightened. 'We'll reorganise along the lines you suggest then, shall we? I don't want to lose your flair and enthusiasm.'

Shelly smiled without mirth. 'And Ross is hopelessly out of his depth and you're beginning to realise that! Sorry, Nathan, but that's a problem all of your own making. You've done me a favour by opening my eyes to what's important and what – frankly – isn't. It's a lesson I shall take with me through life. I presume you won't insist that I work out my notice, in the circumstances? It would embarrass us both.'

Nathan glowered, obviously seeing that he wasn't going to win this battle. 'If that's what you want.'

Within an hour, Shelly was walking along the blue carpeted corridor for the last time, through the imposing chrome reception and out to the car park, her office cleared of her personal possessions. She was surprised to feel no real regret. Where was the zest she used to feel for her job?

Reaching home, she found Ed and Emily finishing lunch. Emily hadn't eaten all of her salad roll but was heavy eyed. She managed a smile for Shelly before clambering to her feet. 'OK if I watch TV, Dad?'

Ed tweaked one of her bunches. 'Of course. The official medical advice is for you to take it easy.'

The crash-bang-wallop soundtrack that accompanied her favourite cartoons soon drifted in from the sitting room. Ed drew his wife closer. 'She'll be asleep on the sofa in thirty seconds. I take it that your appearance here in the middle of the day means that you went ahead with your resignation?'

Shelly slid her arms around him and laid her cheek against the top of his head. 'Yes, it's all over. Nathan was rather shocked. It's probably done him good to learn that loyalty is a two way street.'

'So what next? A new job or an agency of your own? You know the necessary finance is available. In fact...' Ed hesitated. 'I'd like to be involved. No, not to poke my nose in! But I find your work interesting. And I could be useful on the financial side. I'd like to help you succeed.'

Tightening her arms, she breathed in his warmth, touched that he wanted her to be happy and fulfilled – and that he realised that this meant making her own decisions. She had married a good man. They'd come a long way down the road to understanding since his misguided suggestion that she gave up her hard-won position at the agency in order to work for him. 'I know. And if I decide to do that I'd love your help because I've never run an entire business before. But I think that first I'll enjoy some time at home with you and Emily. And when Cliff and Rod are here to talk business I might be able to offer some ideas to promote *Avenue Windows.*'

He pulled her down onto his lap. 'Yes, I'd like us to take more part in each other's lives, instead of just existing stubbornly and rigidly within our own areas. We did too much of that, I think, while we were single parents.'

She plopped a kiss on the end of his nose. 'It's a habit that it will be fun to get out of.'

It was more than a week later that Ed told Emily that he was taking her on an outing.

'Are we going to the hospital?' Still pale, tiredness smudged Emily's eyes. Frowns creased her face more often than smiles these days and Ed wanted to change that. Therapeutic play at home was all very well but he was sure that now she was ready for some gentle stimulus from the outside world.

'Not this time; we're going to see an old friend.'

'Oh?' She brightened. 'Your friend or my friend?'

Ed grinned. 'Your friend – but, I like to think, a kind of family friend, too.'

Emily looked interested. 'Who?' Her school friends, on the advice of the doctors, had only been allowed to visit two at a time and for half-an-hour. Emily was always pleased to see them but never demurred when it was time for them to go. Even small disruptions in routine tired her; it would be months before she was ready to rejoin the hurly burly of school.

'A surprise!' They slid into Ed's car and he stopped to check for traffic at the end of the drive before turning left towards the main road.

It didn't take Emily long to work out where they were going. As they turned out of town, her eyes suddenly shone. 'Junk? Are we going to see Junk?'

'That's right! You recognised the way! Good girl!' Ed beamed at this little step towards the return of old Emily.

When they pulled up in the familiar gateway where long nettles nodded with creamy flowers, Lori, the little girl who was looking after Junk, was preparing to leave with her mother, bubbling with the pleasure of exercising the pony. 'Oh *hello*, Emily! *Thank* you for letting me ride Junk until you're better!' she cried, joyfully. 'He's so sweet, I love him.'

Ed was relieved that he'd thought to agree with Lori's parents that they wouldn't tell Lori about the possibility of eventually buying Junk – Emily was in no way fit for the trauma of knowing her darling was due to get a new owner.

'Thanks for looking after him,' Emily returned. She waited silently while Lori and her mother chattered themselves out and drove off. Finally, she turned to gaze at Junk. The grazing pony's chestnut coat flared brightly in the sunlight, and when he lifted his head he exhibited a pretty white star between his wise brown eyes.

Ed stood back. Emily watched the pony for several minutes before stepping slowly across the grass. But the instant she called, 'Hello, Junk,' Junk's ears swivelled and he ambled forward to greet her as if it were only yesterday she'd last brought him carrots.

Emily ran her hands over his long ears, pausing to scratch his poll. 'Hello, you lovely boy,' and Junk nudged at her with a velvet nose. Emily leant her face against his neck and buried her fingers in his mane.

A lump in his throat, Ed listened to Emily's high voice crooning nonsense to her old friend and the pony whickering in reply. He thought of the days when Emily cantered Junk around the paddock, hair flying, hooves flashing, human and animal moving as one. His heart lifted a little. It would be wonderful to have his daughter smelling of horse again.

After ten minutes he joined Emily, who now had both arms around Junk. 'Nice to see him?' he asked, gently.

Emily nodded, sniffing back tears. Ed dug a tissue from his pocket – it was always a good idea to carry a supply these days. Emily was a bit weepy since her accident. He patted Junk's withers and the smooth part of his back where the saddle went, surprised, as always, at the amount of heat a large animal gave out.

Emily made no move to release the pony from her embrace. 'I thought... I daren't ask about him in case ... in case–'

'I wouldn't have sold him while you were ill.' Ed looked at the white face and tiny frame that belied the courage with which she'd coped with her accident. His heart contracted with love and he found himself saying words he'd never expected to hear himself say. 'You know, I don't see why we shouldn't keep Junk as long as somebody like Lori can be found to exercise him. We'll get a bigger pony for you in a few months when the doctors give us the thumbs up, and he can come and live with Junk. There's room in the stable for one more. Would you like that?'

Silently, shoulders still heaving, Emily unwound her arms from Junk and flung them around her father, nodding violently. He felt his shirt becoming wet beneath her face.

Rocking her in his arms he reflected, a little bitterly, that if he'd allowed himself be persuaded into making this decision months ago instead of letting Emily go on with a pony she'd outgrown, the accident would probably never have happened...

If Chloë had ever dared to dream of her work being awarded space at a London art exhibition, she'd never guessed it would be this soon! Her legs literally shook as they carried her up the grey marble steps of the Thomas Byrne Memorial Art Gallery in Kensington. All the way down on the train and in the unfamiliar billowy warmth of the tube she'd floated in a bubble of unreality. This couldn't be happening to *her*, Chloë Brannigan!

But now she was here and a gentleman in a black suit was asking for her invitation to the private showing at the door, fresh realisation hit her that it *was*.

And it was scary!

'Welcome, Miss Brannigan,' the dark suited man said. He shook her hand. Chloë hardly ever shook hands with anyone and it added to her sensation of strangeness. She hoped her palm wasn't damp. The man held open the door as Chloë, then Kenny, Shelly, Jason, Melissa and Patrick stepped through. 'Won't you join us for refreshments in the Graeme Room?'

The Graeme Room was awesome. Waiters and waitresses moved among the guests with wine, soft drinks, and trays full of canapés. Chloë clutched a glass of cola, but she couldn't eat a morsel. There were little circles of brown bread decorated with prawns, vol-au-vents and, more pragmatically, fingers of pizza, but her tongue was glued to the roof of her mouth. Patrick seemed to be content to eat her share, at least of the pizza.

The atmosphere fizzed with suppressed excitement, families juggling plates of nibbles and glasses of drink and trying to look as if they spent every day in their best clothes standing about in marble halls waiting to see the work of their gifted children exhibited under spotlights. Teenagers raised their voices then hushed one another excitedly. Everyone else seemed to be barely able to stand still, whereas Chloë felt as if she were made of marble, like the columns that stretched up to the lofty ceiling. Still and stiff.

Shelly, Jason, Melissa and Patrick drifted off to inspect an exhibition of African sculpture in one corner but Kenny, glass of wine clutched undrunk in his hand, stuck near Chloë and looked as uncomfortable and close to panic as she felt. 'Well,' he said once, easing his tie. And then, 'Some place, eh?'

Past speech, Chloë nodded.

And then the man in the dark suit who'd manned the door climbed onto a little rise formed by three marble steps and spoke into a microphone. 'I think we're all here, so we can begin.' He introduced himself not as a doorman but as the director of the arts council, 'A position that affords me the privilege of sniffing out the finest young artists in the country.' He smiled, and Chloë's cheeks flamed at his words.

He went on to talk of talent and the ability to work hard – two things that didn't necessarily go hand-in-hand, apparently – promise and potential, and the fulfilling of. Lastly, he talked about opportunity. 'I'd like to offer you the opportunity now of enjoying with me this early viewing of the work of the country's promising young artists. This is their first exhibition. I hope it's the first of many.'

And the arts council director stepped down to swing wide the heavy wooden doors and lead the way into the gallery beyond. The guests followed.

Chloë had been to galleries on school trips and was always quietly thrilled by the respect the pictures received. Space upon a wall that served no other purpose but as a place to hang the work of artists. Sometimes a little rope to prevent people getting too close, as if even *breathing* on the pictures could spoil them. A tile underneath that told the viewer the work's title and who had painted it.

Jason flicked a white leaflet beneath Chloë's nose. 'You're number 28, Chloë.'

Chloë halted. 'What's that?'

'The programme, I picked one up. Look, here's your name, the name of your picture, *A Water World,* and your school and your region. And your picture's number 28 out of 30, alcove M.'

Chloë slipped the paper from Jason's hand to examine her name in print. 'I've got an alcove,' she croaked.

'We'd better go and see where it is then,'

he suggested, linking her arm.

It only took them a few moments. The alcove was a sort of arch with hidden lighting. And there hung her painting in a narrow, natural wood frame, Chloë's name on a white tile beneath.

It was a picture that had particularly pleased Chloë of a corner of the pond at The Old Manse, a frog half out of the water on a large black pebble, golden spears of iris glowing with late afternoon sun, a blush pink water lily, pond-skaters dancing, and, looking out from just below the surface the lugubrious faces of the koi carp, gold and silver, black and orange.

The family arranged itself, smallest in the front rank, and gazed.

Shelly squeezed Chloë's shoulders. Her voice was tight with emotion. 'Well *done,* darling! I'm so *proud.*'

'And me!' Kenny breathed.

'Cool frog,' volunteered Patrick. 'Good 'n slimy.'

'My own thoughts exactly,' came a voice from behind. And Chloë's breath caught to find the arts council director in his smart black suit behind her. 'Very nice. Very nice indeed. Texture, reflection – you've tackled some very tricky stuff. Congratulations,

Chloë – I hope I see a lot more of you.'

'Th-thank you,' managed Chloë. With a smile, the director wandered away.

Chloë's heart beat like eagle's wings inside her ribcage as she gazed at her painting as if she could never get enough of it. She had never been so utterly, fantastically happy in all her life.

The homeward bound train wasn't as busy as the morning one had been, Kenny was glad to discover. He didn't think he could've managed to stand up all the way home, not after the day they'd had. But rush hour had passed as they'd celebrated Chloë's success with a wonderful, fragrant and exotic meal in a China Town restaurant. Chinese food wasn't normally his cup of tea, so to speak, but it had been Chloë's choice and goodness knows she deserved a reward! His eyes prickled with pride every time he thought of her painting up there on the wall of that swanky gallery.

The Wright children gossiped in a group at one side of the rattling train and Kenny, Chloë and Shelly at a table on the other. Chloë, after seeming unable to do much more than squeak at the gallery had been on a high ever since.

'So what did you think of Chinese food then, Dad?' Her eyes gleamed with mischief. She looked beautiful with her dark hair all tumbled around her face, even though she'd put Jason's black jacket on over her blue-patterned dress.

Kenny unknotted his tie, dragged it out of his collar and stuffed it in his pocket. 'I didn't know what I was eating half of the time!'

Shelly grinned. 'You seemed to manage it all right, though.'

'Yes, it was nice, especially that crispy duck affair, with the pancakes. I don't want pie and chips all my life, now do I? It's time I stopped being suspicious of anything foreign.'

The train chucker-chucker-chuckity-chucked along the lines, swaying as it leaned around a curve. Beyond the long windows the soft blues of twilight raced past. Kenny settled deeper into his chair. He felt dead beat after the excitement. Perhaps he'd just rest his eyes for a few minutes…

'Do you wish you'd gone with Philly?'

His eyes opened again to meet his daughter's calm gaze. 'You know that it was never on the cards, Chloë! Me and Philly have got different commitments. Well, no, not *commitments*, more like different ties.'

Chloë wrinkled her nose. 'I don't like

220

being a tie.'

'It's not something you have options about,' Kenny smiled. 'And it's not a case of you tying me. From the moment your mother put you in my arms at the hospital, even when I knew you were on the way, we were tied to *each other,* by love. Love like that isn't a burden, it's a privilege. And it's not that I *can't* leave you while I spend months junketing around the world, or I *mustn't* – it's that I won't! It would hurt me too much. Philly hasn't got any kids so it's not the same for her. OK?'

After a moment Chloë nodded. 'OK. But I still don't feel comfortable that you've given up your happiness for me.'

He snorted. 'It's not "giving up happiness", Chloë. You'll find out for yourself when you're a parent. It's kind of programmed into you. You don't resent it or even think about being any different, and I don't want to be away from you for a long time, so that's that.'

He turned to watch the rocketing scenery as the train rushed through the evening. He wished Chloë hadn't brought this subject up, not today when they were all so happy. It reminded him how much he missed Philly. And missing Philly was something he did plenty, thanks, getting through the days trying to ignore the hollowness he carried in his chest.

'I don't know that it's quite so cut and dried as you make out.' Shelly broke into his thoughts.

Kenny turned in surprise. 'How do you mean?'

She shrugged. 'Why not go out and join Philly just for a little while? Experience some of what's fascinating her, the different lifestyle and the beautiful countryside. Go for a month, say, or six weeks. You don't have to go for a year. You've been a loyal employee at the garage for so many years they're bound to be sympathetic if you ask for a bit of unpaid leave to add to your holiday allowance.'

'Yes, do that,' agreed Chloë, instantly. 'Philly will show you how to use a cyber café! We can keep in touch by e-mail.'

'Can we?' asked Kenny, suspiciously. The nearest he got to a computer was to print invoices out at work.

'You couldn't get to miss me too drastically in a *month*,' insisted Chloë. 'So what's stopping you?'

'A month's a long time.'

'But not *too* long a time.'

Kenny hesitated, almost reluctant to

consider something he'd set his face against months ago. 'It's whether you'd be all right.'

'Of course I would! A month's not like forever, Dad!'

'I don't know.' He rubbed his chin. 'I haven't even got a passport.'

Patting his hand in exaggerated reassurance, Chloë grinned. 'We'll have to get you one.'

'We could've got you one in London this afternoon if he'd brought the right documents!' Shelly winked at him.

'Can you get one in *an afternoon*? Good gracious.' Kenny sat back to mull things over. He *could* take a holiday. He hadn't taken any yet this year. He'd never been properly abroad. Chloë seemed OK about it... He wondered what Philly would say. If she'd be pleased to see him.

He gazed out and wondered what it would be like to see temples and markets and great rivers through a train window instead of fields and the backs of terraced houses. And those funny little taxi cars, of course. Tuk Tuks. He'd like to see them.

Kenny had to deliver Chloë back to The Old Manse from the station because there weren't enough seats in Shelly's car to hold everybody. He was happy to do that but he rather wished that Shelly hadn't refused to take no for an answer about following her into the imposing house to drink posh coffee with her and Ed.

Ed ran down the imposing oak staircase as they entered the lofty hallway. Kenny tried not to feel strange to see how Ed's face lit up at Shelly's greeting smile and how naturally he dropped a kiss on her upturned face.

'So how did the great day go?' Ed demanded of Chloë.

Impulsively, Chloë threw her arms around him. 'Oh Ed! It was magic! I wish you and Emily could've come!'

He beamed. 'Next time, I'll be there.'

The children drifted away to their various rooms, Ed calling after them to remember that Emily was asleep already and Shelly went off to froth the coffee. Kenny was left to be escorted into the sitting room by Ed. They talked for several minutes about Emily's progress. Kenny had heard it all already from the Wright kids but it seemed rude not to enquire.

Then Ed took his turn to make a polite enquiry. 'So, how is Philly? Chloë tells me that she keeps in touch.'

'She seems well.' He hesitated. 'In fact,

Chloë and Shelly between them have more than half-convinced me to go out to spend a month with her in Thailand.'

Shelly pushed her way into the room, bearing the coffee tray. 'You might regret it forever if you don't take the opportunity, Kenny. Oops – sugar!' She put the tray down and dashed back to the kitchen.

Ed looked thoughtful. 'She may be right. We ought to make the most of our opportunities.' Then he added, unexpectedly, 'Philly's a good woman.' He glanced at Kenny. 'Chloë OK about it?'

'She seems to be.' But Kenny felt a worm of uncertainty wriggle in his stomach. Even though he hadn't been able to live with his daughter for the last years he'd always been close to her, geographically, always there to jump in the car if she needed him. 'Although I've never been away from her for a month before...'

'She'll miss you, but she'll have Shelly.'

Kenny paused. Then, diffidently, he said, 'And you.'

Surprise wrote itself on Ed's face. 'I'm not trying to butt in, Kenny–'

'No, you're not. I know that, now. You're just telling me that you'll be there for Chloë if she wants you. And your kids will, too.

Now I've got used to the idea of her having all this extra family, I think it's a good thing.'

A grin of relief spread over Ed's face. 'We do consider her part of the family. She's a good girl and you must've been thrilled for her today.'

Unexpectedly, Kenny felt a lump in his throat. 'Never been so proud in all my life.' He hesitated. 'I'm sorry you couldn't have been there, too.'

Ed had never before touched the world of therapists and was only learning now through Emily's treatment how specialised a field it was, and how valuable to those in need these professionals were as they worked gently with Emily to help her cope with the fiddly everyday tasks that she found difficult and the thickness of speech that was already improving.

Ed was learning, too, to let Emily do things herself, even though the urge to do it for her was itching on the end of his fingers.

This new Emily had no energy and sometimes stared into space. She was likely to appreciate routine, but he was advised to keep therapeutic activities short – not to tire or bore her.

He was ashamed to admit to himself that

the routine bored *him*.

Well, a little tedium was worth it, to have his girl making such progress after an accident when the outcome could've been much worse. Ed knew that the strange feelings of unfamiliarity and loss were due to him grieving for his old life; the clatter and chatter of the factory, the sanctuary of his office, the camaraderie of his colleagues. He desperately missed the freedom to snatch up his jacket and rush from the house to join 'his' world.

Even when he took Emily out for a walk they couldn't go too quickly or too far. She would become querulous with fatigue.

Now that the other children had broken up for the summer holidays he fell into the habit of leaving the walks until Chloë was around. She'd nearly always offer to go along and the time would be beguiled for both he and Emily by her chatter.

Shelly would often join them, too and it pleased him to see her strolling along with Emily, hair shining in the sun.

'You know, not everything about Emily's accident is bad,' he told Chloë as they wandered along the tarmac paths of the park, the trees lending their shade. Both Shelly and Melissa were with Emily, talking about the birdsong. 'I have all this time to spend with my family and my family consists of some wonderful people. You all help with Emily – although Jason is working at the garage several days a week, and Patrick is often playing at friends' houses.'

'He's not allowed to have friends to his own house at the moment,' Chloë reminded him.

Ed grimaced. 'I don't think Emily would have her calm and safe environment the doctors are so keen on with Patrick and his deafening friends roaring about the place!' He held back an overgrowing branch. 'Even Melissa puts aside her own activities for a couple of hours each day to spend time with her sister.'

'Yes. But it's you that does most for Em.' Chloë continued in silence for a minute. 'Ed,' she said, tentatively. 'Would you be able to take a day off? Mum would look after Emily.'

'I suppose so.' He sounded dubious. 'But it doesn't seem fair, does it? Just to take a day off, with nothing particular to do with it.'

'Well, I was wondering… You see, Em can't go because of being so tired. But you could if you wanted to!'

His eyebrows lifted. 'Go where?'

She flushed. 'I wondered if you wanted to

come with me on the school trip to the art exhibition. There are loads of pictures to see, not just mine. You can go into the other galleries and everything. Mum said she'd look after Emily and we...' She flicked him a tentative glance. 'We wondered if you'd like to go. But you don't *have* to, because it is a *school* trip on a bus and everything and with lots of noisy kids and we have to take sandwiches and that's probably not your thing and–' She paused, looking unsure. 'You don't *have* to'

Ed halted mid-stride, a tide of pleasure sweeping through him. He felt as if he'd won a prize. 'But Chloë! There are few things that would please me more!'

Kenny Brannigan wasn't a seasoned traveller. He'd been on a plane precisely twice, there and back to the Channel Island of Jersey with two of his Volkswagen Owners' Club mates. The flight had just been a part of the holiday to be got through, in his opinion, and not much different to being in a bus. But this time he'd spent – he glanced at his watch – eleven hours and twenty-two minutes in the air so far, and the mighty plane was finally making its ponderous descent towards solid ground.

And this time it was going to land in a proper foreign land.

He held onto the seat arms. It wasn't that he was worried about landing, exactly but he always enjoyed a journey more when he was the driver. All around him other passengers continued to read unconcernedly, maybe sucking a sweet to help their ears through the changes in altitude. He was tired. He wasn't one for sleeping upright, like some passengers seemed to be able to. He tried to relax as much as he could with the knowledge racing around his head that he would soon see Philly again. He closed his eyes and conjured up her broad grin and dancing eyes.

It seemed a long time before they were actually down with a small bump and the engine note rose – going into reverse thrust, he thought – and then came the long and tedious process of taxiing, disembarkation, passports, baggage reclaim, all of which involved a lot of traipsing about and standing in queues.

And then finally he was wheeling his case out through a doorway. And there was Philly wearing a bright yellow blouse and a jazzily printed sort of skirt wrapping round and down to her ankles. Her hair was streaked turquoise, and curled into spirals, quite a landmark when so many people around them had flat black glossy hair.

She opened her arms and in a heartbeat he was within them.

'I've missed you!' she whispered.

'Me, too.' His arms tightened.

'I couldn't believe it when you said you would come out here!'

'Me, neither!'

She laughed, pulling back to look up into his eyes. 'And Chloë? Did she really not mind?'

'It was partly her idea.' It seemed from some of the exclamations around them that they might be in the way of other travellers and their luggage but Kenny was intent on his Philly. 'She knows that I've been unhappy at home without you and she said that if I came out for a month it would be a compromise, like, between travelling with you or staying home on my own. I'll miss her, but–' He paused. 'She knows I'll be back.'

Philly kissed him gently. 'And I know too, don't worry.' She grabbed his arm to begin to steer him to the exit. 'Let's find some transport into Bangkok.'

'One of them little Tuk Tuk taxis?' he asked, hopefully.

She burst out laughing. 'What, all the way

into Bangkok? No, we'll get the bus. You can go on a Tuk Tuk tomorrow and the Sky Train and the Pasicharoen Canal boat...'
She chattered excitedly about rice fields and orchid farms, temples and palaces as they found the bus and watched his case safely stowed by a smiling man in loose blue cotton trousers and a white shirt.

She talked nearly all the journey into Bangkok about trips she had planned for him.

He got a word in, eventually, to say what he felt he ought to have been saying more of all along. 'I love you, Philly.'

She paused to search his eyes. 'I love you, too.'

'Are you happy, here?'

Her wonderful smile lit her face. 'Immensely. It's a fabulous place. I'm doing what I always wanted to do, experiencing a different way of life. It's a beautiful country, Kenny.'

'Yes.' He failed to smile.

She dropped her head on his shoulder as the bus hummed into the city and they ended the journey in silence.

The heat and humidity hit Kenny like a hot cloth when they left the air conditioned hotel the next day. The streets were a bustle. The local men wore loose trousers and bright shirts and many of the ladies colour-ful skirts, like Philly's. Over everything was the noise of traffic and chiming voices raised in competition.

He saw his first Tuk Tuk and grinned at the quaint little vehicle blue and silver and with a little advertising hoarding on the rear. In seconds Philly had hailed it and they were on board in the back seats with a wrought iron railing between them and their driver.

Kenny couldn't stop grinning as they trundled along, mainly well behaved traffic, streaming along either side of them, heating the air and stinging his throat with exhaust fumes. 'Funny little thing! It can't make up its mind whether it's a motorbike or a milk float!'

He bent towards Philly and kissed her. 'I want to make the most of every minute here with you.'

She looked up. 'I will be coming home again, you know, Kenny.'

He felt a great lift inside him. 'In a few months? In a year?'

She shook her head, gravely, and heaviness descended on him. Then her amazing grin blazed across her face. 'Much sooner! This is a fantastic country and there are many more fantastic countries to be seen. But maybe not all in one trip! I've discovered something being out here – people are more important than places. So maybe I'll go home when you do, Kenny. Temples and palaces are wonderful but I have a yen to be among old cars and autojumbles again!'

It was about the same time that Chloë found herself again standing in front of her own work – *in a London Gallery! How cool was that?* – Jason and Melissa had asked to come for the second time and were standing back to let Ed, a solid presence beside Chloë, inspect the painting. He gazed at it for a long time. Silently.

Chloë began to feel quite nervous. Perhaps he didn't like it and felt too awkward to say? Perhaps he was still shell-shocked from over two hours on a coach with nearly 50 giggly children singing off key. Perhaps he was struggling to find something kind to say–

'Patrick was right,' he observed, suddenly. 'The frog does look slimy.'

Chloë felt herself going pink with relief. 'Oh! Good.'

'And you've captured the complaining expression of a koi carp wonderfully. They always look as if they're having a good grumble, don't they?' He relapsed again into silent contemplation.

Finally he turned and smiled. 'Chloë, our family has become richer, over the last months.'

Chloë felt herself go pink to puce, this time with embarrassment. She glanced at Jason and Melissa, looking interested at this information. 'You – you don't normally talk about things like that!' she muttered. He was normally so correct about privacy!

He grinned. 'I'm not talking about anything as ordinary as pounds and pence. I mean that my family is richer for having you and your mother in it.'

'Oh!' Her colour subsided.

Ed glanced back at the picture. 'When Shelly and I married I was bewildered by you. You were so indignant when I offered things that I gave to my own children as a matter of course. You dismissed a private school in favour of remaining with your friends, and weren't shy about showing me that you had a dad, thank you very much, and didn't have much use for a spare. I think that was the beginning of a lesson I've learnt recently, about all the things money can't buy.' He nodded at the picture. 'Here's another example – raw talent. You have such a lot!

'But you never show off about it. You have joined my family but you'll never be absorbed by it. You're you – an independent spirit. But the way you give yourself, your time, makes the home we all share a better place.'

Chloë stared down at the floor. 'I like living with you all, now,' she managed, embarrassed all over again.

'We like it, too,' put in Jason.

Melissa grinned. 'Yes, you're not bad.'

Gently, Ed tipped Chloë's face up. 'I'm going to say something that I said before but it didn't go down very well but I hope we know each other better, now. I want to support you through art school.' He held up his hand to stop her from butting in. 'It's not because I'm trying to impress your mother or outdo your dad. It's because I believe in you and I think that facilitating your talent would be a worthwhile thing to do – to help you get on in the world, and to let the world have a look at your work.

'You don't have to make the decision now; it's one for the future. Talk it over with your parents. I just wanted you to know that it's something I want to do, if you'll let me.'

'Sounds good to me,' added Jason.

Chloë looked up into his kindly face and

saw there only a genuine wish to help. His offer wasn't a thinly disguised parading of his wealth. Like a flash she saw that she didn't have to refuse everything Ed Wright's money offered her in order to maintain her own identity or to avoid hurting Kenny's feelings.

She looked at Melissa. She as the one who'd seemed to resent Chloë at first. 'I don't really know–' she began, doubtfully.

But Melissa nodded. 'Go for it.'

Chloë let herself think about it. She was sure her mother had money put by to go towards her education but with Ed's help Chloë could go through art school without a single one of the money worries or arduous evening jobs that formed part of the life of the majority of students. She would leave university without a debt that might take years to repay. She'd be free to concentrate on what was important.

She opened her mouth to thank him but realised he'd fallen into conversation with a couple who'd come up to look at *A Water World*. 'It *is* good, isn't it?' he was saying. 'I'm a fan of the sliminess of the frog, myself.'

Jason drew Chloë forward. 'This is the artist, Chloë.'

'I'm her stepfather,' added Ed. He

squeezed Chloë's hand, briefly. 'I can't tell you how proud all her family is of her.'

'Yes, she's not bad,' said Jason and Melissa in unison.

The couple smiled. 'And brothers and sisters aren't that easy to impress, are they, dear?'

Chloë grinned round. Her family no longer consisted of just her mum and dad, but Jason, Melissa, Patrick and Emily, and, of course, Ed. 'It's brilliant to be part of a big family,' she heard herself agreeing. 'I love it.'